Readers love ANDREW GREY

Half a Cowboy

"…every book captures my interest and gets my emotions going. I am in awe of the fact that he can write so many books and have each one better than the one before…"

—Paranormal Romance Guild

Bad to Be Good

"Grey has a plethora of passages that convey the essence of his characters and the storyline."

—Love Bytes

Paint by Number

"This story, like most of Andrew's books is sweet and full of feelings… If you've never read a book from Andrew Grey and even if you have, I highly recommend this one."

—Open Skye Book Reviews

By Andrew Grey

Accompanied by a Waltz
All for You
Between Loathing and Love
Borrowed Heart
Buried Passions
Catch of a Lifetime
Chasing the Dream
Crossing Divides
Dominant Chord
Dutch Treat
Eastern Cowboy
Hard Road Back
Half a Cowboy
Heartward
In Search of a Story
New Tricks
Noble Intentions
North to the Future
One Good Deed
On Shaky Ground
Paint By Number
The Playmaker
Pulling Strings
Rebound
Rescue Me
Reunited
Running to You
Saving Faithless Creek
Shared Revelations
Survive and Conquer
Three Fates
To Have, Hold, and Let Go
Turning the Page
Twice Baked
Unfamiliar Waters
Whipped Cream

ART
Legal Artistry
Artistic Appeal
Artistic Pursuits
Legal Tender

BAD TO BE GOOD
Bad to Be Good
Bad to Be Worthy

BOTTLED UP
The Best Revenge
Bottled Up
Uncorked
An Unexpected Vintage

BRONCO'S BOYS
Inside Out • Upside Down
Backward
Round and Round
Over and Back
Above and Beyond

THE BULLRIDERS
A Wild Ride
A Daring Ride
A Courageous Ride

BY FIRE
Redemption by Fire
Strengthened by Fire
Burnished by Fire
Heat Under Fire

CARLISLE COPS
Fire and Water • Fire and Ice
Fire and Rain • Fire and Snow
Fire and Hail • Fire and Fog

Published by DREAMSPINNER PRESS
www.dreamspinnerpress.com

By Andrew Grey

CARLISLE DEPUTIES
Fire and Flint
Fire and Granite
Fire and Agate
Fire and Obsidian
Fire and Onyx
Fire and Diamond

CHEMISTRY
Organic Chemistry
Biochemistry
Electrochemistry
Chemistry Anthology

DREAMSPUN DESIRES
The Lone Rancher
Poppy's Secret
The Best Worst Honeymoon Ever

EYES OF LOVE
Eyes Only for Me
Eyes Only for You

FOREVER YOURS
Can't Live Without You
Never Let You Go

GOOD FIGHT
The Good Fight
The Fight Within
The Fight for Identity
Takoda and Horse

HEARTS ENTWINED
Heart Unseen
Heart Unheard
Heart Untouched
Heart Unbroken

HOLIDAY STORIES
Copping a Sweetest Day Feel
Cruise for Christmas
A Lion in Tails
Mariah the Christmas Moose
A Present in Swaddling Clothes
Simple Gifts
Snowbound in Nowhere
Stardust
Sweet Anticipation

LAS VEGAS ESCORTS
The Price • The Gift

LOVE MEANS…
Love Means… No Shame
Love Means… Courage
Love Means… No Boundaries
Love Means… Freedom
Love Means … No Fear
Love Means… Healing
Love Means… Family
Love Means… Renewal
Love Means… No Limits
Love Means… Patience
Love Means… Endurance

Published by DREAMSPINNER PRESS
www.dreamspinnerpress.com

By Andrew Grey

LOVE'S CHARTER
Setting the Hook
Ebb and Flow

PLANTING DREAMS
Planting His Dream
Growing His Dream

REKINDLED FLAME
Rekindled Flame
Cleansing Flame
Smoldering Flame

SENSES
Love Comes Silently
Love Comes in Darkness
Love Comes Home
Love Comes Around
Love Comes Unheard
Love Comes to Light

SEVEN DAYS
Seven Days
Unconditional Love

STORIES FROM THE RANGE
A Shared Range
A Troubled Range
An Unsettled Range
A Foreign Range
An Isolated Range
A Volatile Range
A Chaotic Range

STRANDED
Stranded • Taken

TALES FROM KANSAS
Dumped in Oz • Stuck in Oz
Trapped in Oz

TALES FROM ST. GILES
Taming the Beast
Redeeming the Stepbrother

TASTE OF LOVE
A Taste of Love
A Serving of Love
A Helping of Love
A Slice of Love

WITHOUT BORDERS
A Heart Without Borders
A Spirit Without Borders

WORK OUT
Spot Me • Pump Me Up
Core Training
Crunch Time
Positive Resistance
Personal Training
Cardio Conditioning
Work Me Out Anthology

Published by Dreamspinner Press
www.dreamspinnerpress.com

ANDREW GREY

Rescue Me

Published by
DREAMSPINNER PRESS

5032 Capital Circle SW, Suite 2, PMB# 279,
Tallahassee, FL 32305-7886 USA
www.dreamspinnerpress.com

This is a work of fiction. Names, characters, places, and incidents either are the product of author imagination or are used fictitiously, and any resemblance to actual persons, living or dead, business establishments, events, or locales is entirely coincidental.

Cover content is for illustrative purposes only and any person depicted on the cover is a model.

Mass Market Paperback ISBN: 978-1-64108-256-3
Trade Paperback ISBN: 978-1-64405-887-9
Digital ISBN: 978-1-64405-886-2
Mass Market Paperback published May 2022
v. 1.0

Printed in the United States of America

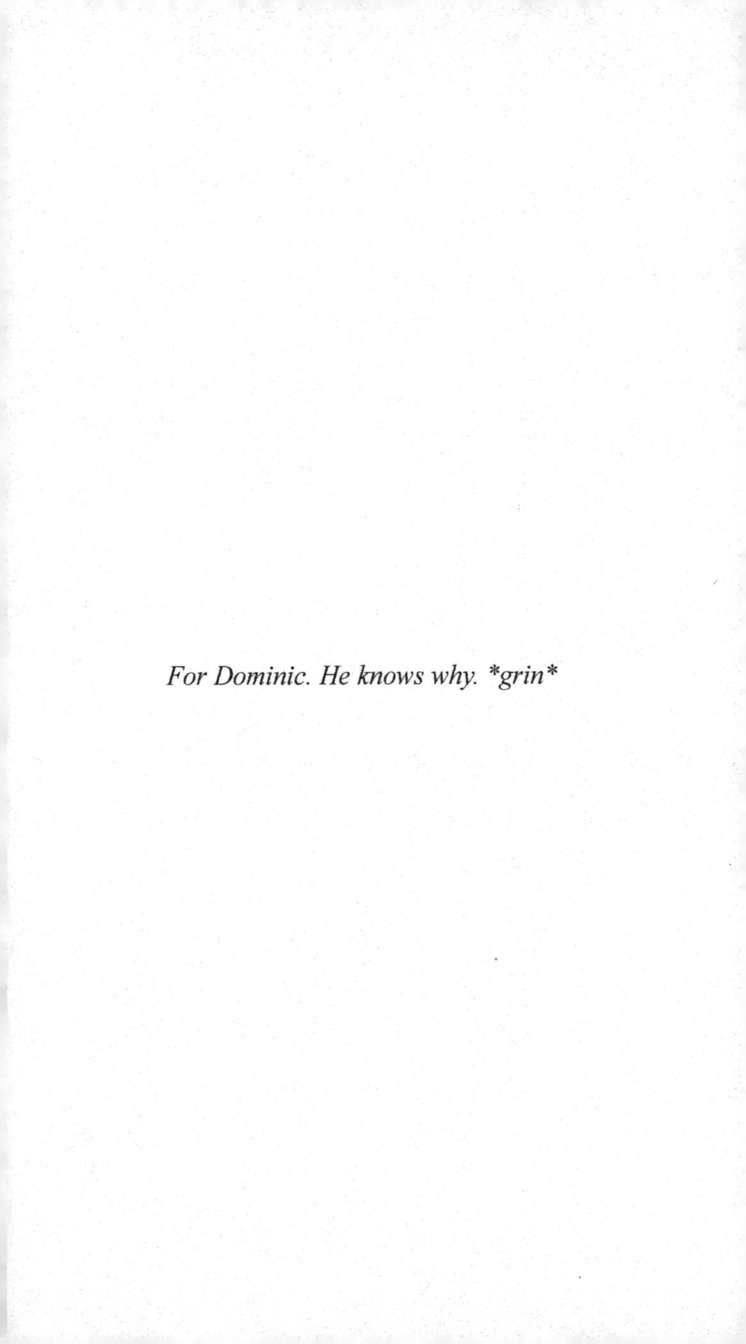

For Dominic. He knows why. *grin*

Chapter 1

"OKAY GUYS, I'm coming," Mitchell called as he opened the door to what had once been the low barn of the family farm. Few things made him happier than the barks and cries that started when he slid the door open first thing in the morning. "Everyone is going to get brekkie and no one will be left out, I promise," he said to calm the rabble, but it had no effect. He slid the door closed, smiled, and opened two of the cages so the dogs could run around his legs as he went to start preparing the food. They jumped around him, tails wagging. *Come play with us.* Mitchell scratched their heads and got to work, the dogs occupying themselves until he set down the bowls. They both attacked their food, eating and drinking, happy dogs. And Mitchell loved all fifteen of them.

Once Bowser and Bruno were fed, he let the two young labs out into a play yard and went about feeding the others. Those he could, he put with the labs so they could run and play. The newer arrivals he kept isolated in case of disease. And there were a few, like Jasper, who didn't get along well with other dogs. He fed him separately but paid him just as much attention as he did the others. These boys and girls were like his family.

"Knock, knock," a deep voice said from the doorway.

"Careful," Mitchell called back to the stranger. "Don't let any of them out." He believed in letting the dogs run and play as much as possible. He scooped up Randi before she could make a break for it. She was a little Chihuahua mix, lightning fast, and loved to try to make a run for it. He soothed her with pets as the door opened slowly and a man of about forty, in tan pants and a blue shirt and carrying a clipboard, stepped inside. He closed the door behind him.

"Well…," he said as he looked around. "What have we here?"

"I need to finish feeding," Mitchell said. He put a bowl out for the final dog and then put the old St. Bernard into one of the runs so he could either get some exercise or, more likely, take a nap. "What can I help you with?"

The man sighed. "There's been a complaint about the barking."

"I see. Let me guess—from the people who moved in over there." He pointed toward the now butter-yellow house on the other side of his. "They moved in two months ago and have called me three times because of the dogs. I've been running this shelter here for four years now. I was here first and I'm not going to stop." He put his hands on his hips.

"They apparently have a baby and—"

"Then they should have thought of that before buying the place," Mitchell interrupted. "I have fifteen dogs—" He stopped. "Maybe you should start by telling me who you are?"

"Clark Fenner. I'm with codes compliance at Carlisle Borough. We received a complaint about barking, and they claimed that the dogs were left unattended for long hours, that they weren't being fed properly, and that you had fighting dogs."

"Mitchell Brannigan, and my dogs are all well cared for. They're fed and well exercised. And I have a few *former* fighting dogs." He took Clark over to one of the runs. "This is Bosco. He was rescued a few weeks ago from a place in Lancaster. Bosco was injured badly in a dog fight. The police over there raided the place, and one of them called me. I picked him up and brought him here. Bosco is a good dog when people are around, but he's aggressive with other dogs. I keep him isolated from the others and am working with him. He may never be comfortable around other dogs, but I'm hoping to help him to behave better so he can be adopted out. Right now I'm near the cap of what I can handle, but I have three dogs being adopted out today and two more couples coming in tomorrow."

Clark narrowed his gaze. "How do you make money at this?" he asked.

"I don't. This is a nonprofit." Mitchell continued petting Randi; she calmed him down. He had considered adopting her himself. But then, he wanted to do that with all the dogs, and he'd long ago told himself that he needed to keep a distance or else his house would be as full as the shelter. "I'm also a veterinarian, and my practice is a mile up the road. I have regular office hours, and during those times, the dogs are in their cages. I know they bark sometimes, but it's a fact of life. These dogs are good dogs, and they are cared for. All have their shots, and I would never allow any of my dogs to be abused in any way, least of all used for fighting."

Clark's expression softened. "I see." He looked around once more. "I wasn't informed of that." He peered into some of the cages and then looked out into the yard at the runs where the dogs were playing. "Dang, that one's a beauty." He stopped in the doorway.

"Rex… yeah, he is. His family got him as a pup and thought they could handle taking care of him. He's a giant schnauzer and weighs about seventy-five pounds." Mitchell opened the door to the run. "Come here, Rex," he said gently, and the large black dog approached and nuzzled right in for pets. "He was too much once they had a baby, so I took him." Clark stroked him. "He's wonderful and incredibly affectionate. Rex has been with me for almost six months now."

"How long do you keep them?" Clark asked.

Mitchell stared, tensing. "Until they're adopted. I don't put dogs down here for any reason other than illness. There is no such thing as a bad dog, just bad pet parents. Rex will be with me until he finds a home. They all will."

Rex approached Clark, and soon he sat right next to him as Clark petted and talked to him softly.

"I have a fenced-in backyard in town, and my wife spends a lot of time alone during the day while I'm working. Would it be okay if I brought her over later to meet Rex here?" He knelt down, and Rex practically put his head on Clark's shoulder, soaking in the attention.

Mitchell knew that look, and he turned away, smiling, because he knew Rex had likely found a home. That spark when a dog and person clicked was definitely there.

"That would be great. Please take some pictures of your yard, and I'll have some paperwork for you to fill out when you come back, and I can explain the adoption fees. I want to make sure you understand how to care for him. Of course he's had all his shots, and I have his records. If you adopt one of my dogs, then I give a discount on all vet care for the rest of the dog's life." He was going to be sad to see Rex go, but if it was to a good home, then that was the best thing.

Clark smiled brightly. "Thank you." He continued petting Rex, and Mitchell had a pretty good idea that he was falling in love. That sort of thing was a lot easier with dogs than it was with people. Dogs gave love no matter what, and they did it without regard to looks or taste or whether you happened to snore. And dogs certainly had a sense about people… something

Mitchell sorely wished he could borrow. His history of relationships left a lot to be desired, and he much preferred the company of animals to that of people. At least he understood their motives.

"I'll be back with my wife. I'm sure she's going to be as taken with him as I am." Clark took a few pictures and sent them off, and his phone chimed a few seconds later. Clark rolled his eyes and messaged back. "She says she's wanted a dog for years and was waiting for me to come around. So I guess if you'll hold him for us, we'll come around later and get him."

"Wonderful," Mitchell said. He went to the office and pulled out the papers he required, along with a list of supplies he recommended for a dog like Rex. "Here is the information I need filled out. Also a list of supplies and the kind of food he's on. When you come back, I'll talk to both of you about his care." This was a banner day as far as he was concerned. "I take it there's no problem with the shelter."

"None. I'll address the complaint at the borough and close it as baseless. I would suggest you might want to see if you can talk to your neighbor. Try to get to know them a little. Maybe if they understand what you're doing, you can patch things up."

What Clark said made sense. Mitchell needed to figure out how to smooth things over with his neighbor.

MITCHELL CLOSED up the clinic and then stopped at the shelter to feed all of the dogs and get them in for the night. As usual, he was greeted with y[illegible] barks, and wagging tails. He started the process for evening feeding as a car pulled into the drive, followed by another, and then a third. Mitchell greeted his visitors and reviewed the care of their new pets with each of them before waving goodbye as three of his dogs found new homes. Once the shelter was quiet again, he finished feeding and brushed Rex so he looked good when Clark and his wife stopped by. He was truly sad to see him go, but the way Rex perked up when he heard Clark's voice, and then the excitement when his wife saw him, sent a jolt of joy racing through his heart.

"He's beautiful."

"Isn't he?" Mitchell said as he led Rex out on a leash. He went right up to her and nuzzled in, and she began petting him like Rex was a long-lost friend.

"We'll take him, of course," she said. "Clark has all the paperwork done, and we have the supplies in the trunk. And because he's so big, we got him a raised water and food bowl as well as a bunch of toys." She took the leash, and Rex practically pranced as she walked him around the yard outside the shelter. "Is there anything else we need to do?" she asked brightly.

"I don't think so. Not right now. Just make sure he has a bed or he'll want to sleep on yours, and Rex will take up most of the space." He smiled, and they nodded. They both shook his hand before they left the shelter. Mitchell watched them go and went back closed up the shelter for the night, and headed to the house.

Mitchell figured he could eat once he got back, so he packed up the cookies that one of his patients had brought to the clinic, checked himself in the mirror, and then headed up the street to the neighbors' for a visit.

He wasn't quite sure what to expect. He knew someone was home. He'd seen a man out in the yard a few times, but mostly the place seemed buttoned up and quiet. Still, he strolled along the road and then up the drive and the walk, to the front door, where he knocked softly. He heard movement inside and was about to ring the bell when the door opened and a haggard man in his midthirties, the same as Mitchell, stared at him. A baby wailed on his shoulder. "I'm sorry, did I wake the baby?"

The man shook his head. His hair was all askew and his brown eyes half-lidded, lips drawn into a line, and his skin a little sallow, like he was too tired to move. Still, he was handsome under all the dishevelment, with a granite jaw and high cheekbones. "No. She's been fussy all night." Mitchell held up the plate of cookies, and the man pushed open the door. "Come on in. I hope she'll wear herself out soon." He patted her back, and the little thing fussed and sniffled.

"Is she sick?"

"I don't know. She doesn't have a fever, but she keeps pulling up her legs and cries like crazy. The doctor says she's losing weight, so I feed her whenever she's hungry, but the little thing doesn't have an appetite." He was clearly worried sick and at his wits' end. "I'm Beau, by the way. Beau Pfister."

"Mitchell Brannigan. I have the farm next to you." He wasn't going to hide who he was. That wasn't the way to start things off with a neighbor.

"The one with the dogs? How many do you have over there, anyway? I just get her down to sleep and they bark, and she wakes… it's…."

"At the moment, twelve. I adopted out three today. I run a shelter out of the old barn. I insulated it and made a good home for them in there. Basically, I rescue the dogs that no one else seems to want and find them good homes. I'm also the vet with the office up the road."

The little girl took the opportunity to wail once again and then farted, except she did more than that.

"Excuse me, I need to change her." Beau made a stink face. "I'll be right back. Have a seat if you like." He raced away.

Mitchell set the cookies on the table and automatically folded the blankets strewn over one end of the sofa. Then he sat down to wait. At least the baby had stopped fussing.

"Sorry," Beau said when he came back, a quiet baby in his arms.

"No need. I understand. The hard part is that she can't tell you what's wrong." Mitchell understood that. His professional life would be so much easier if he were Dr. Doolittle. "Can I ask what she's eating?"

"Formula. Her mother, Amy, is… *was* my best friend, and she named me Jessica's guardian in case something happened." He leaned forward, holding his head in his hands. "How was I supposed to know some drunk driver would hit her on her way home from work?"

"I'm sorry. How long have you had Jessica?"

"Just over three weeks, I guess."

Mitchell sighed. "Why don't you show me what you're feeding her. Was she being breastfed prior to that?"

Beau hefted himself out of the chair. "No. Amy couldn't, so Jessica was always on formula, and I got the same kind." He brought back two containers. One was empty and the other half full. "I kept this one so I'd know what to get."

Mitchell saw the issue almost immediately. "This is what she was eating before?" he asked, just to be sure, and Beau nodded. "Then it's the formula. Get this exact same kind in the orange container. This is lactose-free. I bet little Jessica has a milk sensitivity and the lactose is upsetting her tummy. Does she always have explosive diapers?"

Beau nodded.

"That would explain it. Change her formula. I bet her appetite will come back when her tummy doesn't hurt, and her diaper changes won't be as messy."

"Are you sure?" Beau asked.

Mitchell shrugged. "I'm not a doctor, I'm a vet. But a lot of what goes into various creatures and people makes a huge difference in their lives and health." He showed Beau the label. "This is lactose-free, and what you're using isn't."

Beau sighed. "To tell you the truth, I'd give just about anything for her to sleep for a few hours. Maybe then I could do the dishes or just take a nap." He yawned and sat back in the chair. Mitchell was afraid Beau was going to drop off to sleep any second.

"Maybe I should go and let you rest. I just wanted to stop by and say hello." He didn't go into defusing the situation about the dogs. He didn't want to bring that up.

"I'm glad you stopped. It's been nice to talk to someone who can talk back." Beau half smiled. "And thank you for the cookies. It's been so long since I ate anything that didn't come out of the freezer and the microwave, I think I've forgotten what real food tastes like." He opened the door, and Mitchell got set to leave.

"Then why don't you and Jessica come over for dinner sometime? My cooking isn't gourmet, but most people find it edible, and a lot of what I cook I learned from my mother. If you want home cooking, I can manage that." He smiled.

"Are you sure?" Beau asked. "A lot of the time, Jessica gets fussy and I need to take care of her. I used to have a lot of friends, but most of them don't know what to make of me with her, so they call and stuff, but the nights we used to get together have turned into story time, diaper changes, and bottles. Even the ones who had kids, theirs are older now and they have their own lives." He shrugged. "But if you're serious, I'd be happy to come to dinner."

Mitchell stepped out into the late evening air. The last of the summer light was just fading as he turned toward home. "Stop by tomorrow. I usually get home about six, and I have to feed the dogs. So about seven will work."

"I'll see you then," Beau said and closed the door.

Mitchell headed for home, wondering what he was going to make for dinner tomorrow. At least he seemed to have patched things up with his handsome neighbor.

Chapter 2

BEAU TOOK advantage of Jessica's late afternoon nap to finish up the project he'd been struggling with and sent it off to his boss at Dickinson College. He had been developing a new distance-learning program to help students learn to use the college library and do in-depth research. Usually this information was presented to the students in a library-based class, but this would free up staff for other tasks, and the students could learn at their own pace. At least that was the idea. With that project complete, he sat back, smiled, and enjoyed the momentary quiet… until Jessica's whimpery cries came through the baby monitor.

He hurried in to get her before she could get a good wind under her sails. He changed her and then made up a bottle of her new formula, which he gave her just as she was pulling in the air for a really good wail. "You and I are going to the neighbor's for dinner," he told her. "So I want you to be on your best behavior. That means no exploding diapers and maybe a nice long nap while we're there." He looked down at her huge blue eyes, which stared back at him. "Maybe we can find you something special to wear." He carried her out of the kitchen to her little bedroom and opened the closet, but before he could pick an outfit, the doorbell rang. Beau had been here two months without so much as a visitor, and now two days in a row?

He opened the door and glared at Gerome. "What are you doing here?" he asked as lightly as he could so he didn't disturb Jessica, even as he seethed inside.

Gerome lowered his gaze to Jessica, who was just finishing her bottle. "What the hell is that?" He muscled his way past Beau and into the living room. Beau closed the door. "I see it's true. You moved out here to the country. How butch of you." Gerome put his hands on his hips. Beau's ex-husband was huge but could swish with the best of them. "I found out where you were living and had a meeting in Harrisburg, so I figured I'd stop by to see if you've come to your senses yet." Gerome was a fun guy, but he lived in a world of his own making. That worked for him and his art. Gerome made huge metal sculptures. They were intricate and beautifully flowing. But it didn't work for Beau—especially when *fun* and *artistic* meant coming home to find the studio assistant fucking the hell out of his husband in his and Beau's marital bed.

"I came to my senses, as you call it, as soon as I found you—" He stumbled over the word he wanted to use because he didn't swear in front of Jessica.

"—in bed with someone else." He turned away. "Have you moved out of the house and studio yet?" he asked. "It's mostly mine, and I want it all sold." Maybe he was being petty, but Beau had no intention of spending the next part of his life financially tangled with Gerome.

"Come on," Gerome wheedled. He was good at that. "You know you miss me...."

Jessica whimpered, and Beau put her over his shoulder to burp her. She gurgled and rested her head on his shoulder before burping loud enough to make a sailor proud.

"That's my girl," he said softly. "And as for you, I'm done. The divorce is final, I have a new life here, and as per the agreement, the property is to be sold."

Gerome drew nearer, looming over him. "But I work in the studio, and you know how hard it is to find affordable space in Philadelphia. I need some—"

Beau shook his head. "Then buy me out according to the agreement you signed when we bought the property and what was agreed on in the divorce. By my estimate, it's 1.8 million." That felt good. Yeah, he was being a little bitchy, but Gerome had really shattered his heart. Beau had thought the talented man in front of him was the one, that he and Gerome would spend their lives together. He'd put most of the inheritance from his grandparents into the house and studio property, though thankfully he had thought to specify how the property was to be owned before he married Gerome.

"I don't have that kind of money," Gerome whined.

"Then I'll contact a realtor friend tomorrow to list the property. You need to find a separate place to live and vacate the studio. Any damage will be taken from your share of the proceeds." He was well aware of how vindictive and petty Gerome could be. This entire situation had gone on long enough. "Now please leave. I'm not coming back to you." He pointed toward the door as Jessica began to fuss. He gave her the remainder of the bottle.

"What's with the baby?"

"Amy died. I sent you a note a few weeks ago. I'm raising Jessica." Gerome never paid attention to anything that didn't have to do with him. "Now, we have places to go, and you're going to make us late." He let Gerome open the door, and as soon as he stepped outside, Beau kicked it closed.

"I'm sorry, sweetheart. I used to be married to him, but you can be thankful that he isn't going to be your daddy." Beau didn't think he could handle two babies at the same time.

Jessica was awake and playful as he dressed her. Then he put her on the floor under some hanging toys and packed the diaper bag. Once he was ready, he lifted her, in her carrier, and the bag and walked over to the neighbor's. Jessica loved to be out for walks and calmed immediately. Beau hoped that she didn't fall asleep too soon.

Their arrival was greeted by the call of the wild. Mitchell came out of the barn. "That's enough, guys.

Cool it," he called and pulled the barn door partway closed. Then he turned to Beau, his smile setting Beau's insides aflutter, chasing away the last of the darkness that Gerome had left in his wake. The flush of energy and the way Mitchell looked at him had Beau's cheeks heating, and he wished he could hide until it went away. "Come on inside. They'll settle down in a few minutes, unless you'd like to go see them. Most of the pack would love a visitor."

Beau wasn't so sure of that, but he nodded anyway, set the diaper bag just inside the door, and followed Mitchell out to the barn.

"These are all the dogs I have at the moment. I adopted out three more today, so I'm down to eleven." The delight in Mitchell's expression tamped down some of Beau's nerves. "Fifteen is about all I can handle."

All the dogs seemed excited. Some bent down, butts in the air and tails wagging, hoping to be played with. Other were quiet and standoffish. Small dogs, large dogs, ones of all descriptions, for the most part tails wagging so rapidly they might have caused a breeze. "I don't think I've ever seen so many of them all in one place." He positioned Jessica into his arms so she could see. Mitchell let two of the dogs out and picked up a small one.

"This is Randi, and that's Sweetiepie. Sometimes they come named, and other times I do it. Randi is really sweet. I'm surprised she hasn't been adopted."

Beau slowly reached out and stroked her head. "What happened to her?"

"Lawn mower. Her owner was careless and cut her. He brought her into the clinic and asked me to put her to sleep. I just couldn't. So I took her and did the surgery to close up her wounds, nursed her to health, then brought her here." Mitchell stroked her body as Beau reached down to pet Sweetiepie, a brindle bulldog mix who was just as gentle as could be.

"And this one?" It was pretty obvious, judging by the myriad of wagging tails around him and the state of these pups, that Mitchell had a huge heart. It would take one to do what he'd done. It occurred to Beau that most people would have been like Randi's former owner and written a lot of these dogs off. Hell, he might have been one of those people. Beau would like to think he wasn't, but never having had a pet, he didn't know. Still, to care that much took a special kind of person. Too bad they were really rare, at least in Beau's experience.

"Broken leg that festered. I had to remove it, but she does well on three legs and is as gentle as can be. I refuse to let any of them be uncared for." Mitchell's gaze grew hard for a moment and then softened again. "I started the shelter a few years ago as an accompaniment to the clinic. I couldn't bear putting down or sending dogs that needed help to one of the other shelters. So after I inherited the property here, I leased out the land to the neighbor on the other side of your place and converted the old storage barn into a shelter. I added runs and secure outdoor spaces for them. In the clinic, I have pictures of the dogs up for adoption, and I work with groups and law enforcement to rescue dogs in trouble." It was pretty clear from the way he spoke that Mitchell really felt for and connected with the dogs in his care.

Beau continued stroking Sweetiepie's head as Jessica watched the dogs, drooling and chewing on her fingers. "This is pretty amazing. I had no idea. I mean, you see those commercials on TV, but you never know how much of that is real or just for the cameras." His gaze roved over the large enclosures, each housing a dog. He stepped closer, and a basset hound with gentle eyes scooted up to him, tail wagging slowly.

Mitchell patted Sweetiepie and gently put her back in her cage. Then he did the same with Randi. "It's real. People do terrible things to one another, and sometimes they treat their dogs the same way." He stepped back, and Beau followed him out of the shelter, letting Mitchell close the door. "I don't think I could live with myself if I ignored what I saw."

Mitchell led the way across the yard, staying close, and then held the door for Beau to go ahead. Beau couldn't help thinking about those dogs, but his mind spent more time turning over his thoughts on their rescuer, and he couldn't help taking a peek at the way Mitchell filled out the tight jeans that gripped his thighs and cradled his rear end.

A wave of heat welled up inside him, and Beau wasn't quite sure what to do with it. Oh, he knew what it meant, along with the way his pulse raced.

There was something attractive about the dog-rescuing veterinarian, Beau couldn't deny that. But for three weeks, his attention had been on Jessica, work, and getting through the day. He didn't have time for anything else. Hell, for weeks Beau had figured that the sexy part of his life was over, at least for the next eighteen years or so. Maybe forever. A good night's sleep sounded like heaven right about now, never mind anything more strenuous in bed.

Beau pulled his straying thoughts back to the here and now.

Jessica snuffled and fussed as soon as he was inside, and Beau got a prepared bottle out of the bag. He checked the temperature of the bottle and gave it to her.

"Are you seeing a difference?" Mitchell asked.

"Yeah. She's hungry all the time, and a lot of the fussiness has disappeared." He sat down on the sofa, and Mitchell sat with him. "I change her a lot now because of all she's eating, but at least I'm not trying to get her to eat all the time." He sighed and sat back. "Would you like to hold her?"

Beau took the bottle and transferred Jessica to the crook of Mitchell's arm. Jessica watched Mitchell as she ate, holding his finger when he offered it.

"You're beautiful, little one, yes you are. And hungry too." Mitchell removed the bottle. Beau handed him a burp rag as he patted her back on his shoulder.

"Does she always belch like that?" Mitchell asked as Beau cleaned up the little bit of mess.

Mitchell held her once again, rocking slightly. "I think things need to settle a little and then she'll be ready for some more." He wagged his fingers in front of her, and she held them before smiling. "Dang, you are a beauty."

"She takes after her mommy." Beau sat back and blinked, trying not to wipe his eyes. "Amy was stunning. Could have been a model."

"What about Jessica's father?" Mitchell asked.

Beau shrugged. "He isn't in the picture. I know his name is Ronald van der Spoel because I have the documents she had where he signed away his rights to her. He isn't going to be involved at all." That was a huge relief. The last thing Beau wanted was someone showing up with a claim to his daughter. He might have only had Jessica for three weeks, but she was his last connection to Amy, and he loved her. Jessica already felt like his own daughter, and the thought of giving her up now, for any reason, made his heart threaten to shatter.

Jessica fell asleep in Mitchell's arms, and he smiled, watching her. "I was an only child and the youngest of all the cousins, so I never really spent much time around babies," he said as he rocked his arms slowly. "At least baby people. I helped birth my first horse when I was nine. Dad said I did a good job and then gave me the colt. I raised him, helped train him, and learned to ride him. He's out in the pasture now, retired and happy. He's the last of the horses on the property, and he'll stay until he dies."

Beau got comfortable. "So you've been around animals your entire life?"

Mitchell smiled and nodded slowly, not breaking the rhythm of his slow movements. "Oh yeah. I had the full complement of pets and animals. Once I even had a pet pig. Mom had a fit about that one because she'd gotten him to raise and slaughter." He grinned. "Mom had visions of bacon and ham, and I had visions of Wilbur from *Charlotte's Web*. In that case, Mom won, but I refused to eat pork for a year just in case it came from Wellington." Mitchell chuckled. "I also had a pet goat, dogs, and cats. I raised a steer and other livestock. No chickens, though. Didn't care for them."

Jessica yawned and stretched before settling easily in Mitchell's arms again.

"Do you want me to take her?" Beau asked quietly. Part of him was grateful for the break, and yet he felt itchy that he wasn't holding her. It was weird.

"I like holding her. It's different for me, and she's warm and so cute." He rocked her gently, with Jessica sleeping away. "Did you have any animals growing up?"

Beau shook his head. "None. My mom was allergic to everything. She was one of those people who had allergies to all animals, so I didn't have any dogs or cats. Even if I went to a friend's who had them, I had to change my clothes and put them in the washer as soon as I came home. It was pretty bad."

Mitchell gaped at him. "No pets at all?"

Beau shook his head, looking at him like he was the most deprived person on earth. It was just the way things had been, and Beau hadn't known anything else. Sure, he had wanted to have a dog, but unlike most kids, where they kept asking and eventually wore their parents down, there had been no chance of that happening. Beau had just had to accept it.

Mitchell slowly leaned forward and passed him Jessica. "I'll be right back."

He left by the front door and passed quickly in front of the window. Beau wondered where he was going, but he returned a few minutes later with something in his arms. When he came back inside, Mitchell put Randi down on the floor. The little dog ran over to him, and Beau tensed a little. It was one thing to be around the dogs out in the barn, but he felt his arms tighten slightly around Jessica as Randi jumped onto the sofa and sniffed her blanket.

"Is this going to be okay?" Beau asked.

Mitchell chuckled. "Randi is sweet, and there's nothing aggressive about her." The blanket fell away from one of Jessica's feet, and before Beau could cover it, Randi sniffed her and gave her a lick, then settled on the sofa.

"Was she tasting her?" Beau asked, unsure if he should be concerned.

"Maybe a little. Dogs explore their world differently from us. We use touch and sight a lot. Dogs see a more limited range of color than we do, and while they do use visual cues, they also explore with their nose and tongue. That's all she was doing, right, girl?" Mitchell sat on the other side of Randi, who was watching Jessica, her head on her paws. He petted her, but Beau noticed that her attention stayed on Jessica. He wasn't too sure how he felt about that.

"Let me check on dinner." Mitchell got up.

Beau hoped that the dog would follow him out of the room, but Randi stayed on the sofa without moving. He tentatively scratched her head, and she leaned into the touch, obviously wanting more, but she didn't come any closer, and when he stopped, she lay back down.

"It will be about twenty minutes. I made a Hawaiian chicken recipe. It's got rice and pineapple. It's not fancy, but if you don't like that sort of thing, I can find you something else…." Mitchell seemed nervous, but the chicken scent reached Beau's nose, and he was suddenly really hungry. His stomach rumbled, and he nodded.

"It sounds good." He liked pineapple, and chicken was always a winner. "I've been existing on food I can microwave for so long, a home-cooked meal is going to seem like heaven. You know that Jessica hasn't been sleeping or eating very well, so I was up a lot with her."

Mitchell chuckled slightly. "Then you move in next to fifteen dogs whose barking woke her up just when you got her to sleep."

Beau felt like such a heel for calling the authorities on Mitchell. "I was sleep-deprived and at my wits' end, I guess. She cried and cried and was so upset all the time. I swear I existed on two or three hours of sleep for days. Last night was the first time she slept four hours in a row since I got her, and that was heaven. I fed and changed her, and she went right back to sleep. It was a miracle." He sighed. "You really saved my life with the whole lactose thing. That really made a difference." Beau actually felt sane and much more normal. It was like he could see the light of day for the first time in weeks. "I was starting to worry that I was the worst daddy in the world and that maybe I shouldn't be the one to take care of her." What if he messed up and hurt her somehow? There was still so much he didn't know, and he was trying to learn on the job, but this was so much more intense than he could ever have imagined. His nerves and doubts kicked in again. "Though she's eating like a trooper now."

"She's happy, and her belly doesn't hurt." Mitchell stroked the dog between them. "She's a good little girl, and you're very lucky. I always wanted a child, but I doubt that's in the cards. Most of the guys that I dated would chew off their right arm before deciding to have children."

Beau grinned. He had suspected, from the vibes he got, that Mitchell might be gay. It was good to know that his instincts weren't gone and that his gaydar wasn't dead.

"My now ex-husband stopped by before I came over. He actually asked me if I'd come to my senses yet. I know he wants me back, but I have no intention of returning to the controlling jerk."

"How long ago did you leave?" Mitchell asked, leaning closer. His earthy scent caught Beau's nose, and he closed his eyes, stifling a groan because dang, that was good and went right to his belly. For a second he thought it might have been the food, but food never got him hard. Heck, he had actually started to think that having Jessica had killed any sex drive he might have had. Beau now understood pretty clearly why he had heard that the best birth control was having children. He wondered how parents actually had the energy for sex. Beau sure didn't right now.

"About a year ago, I had to get out of my own house. It was over before that, but I didn't pull the plug and I should have." He moved Jessica to his other arm to give himself a rest. "I think I stayed because I hoped things would get better. But it got worse. If I went out with friends, he called and texted all the time. It was twenty questions when I got home."

Mitchell leaned forward. "Did yours hit you?" The way Mitchell said the words sent a chill through him and made him wonder how Mitchell had gotten himself into that situation. Beau understood how it happened to him. Shame burned inside that he hadn't seen how Gerome really was much earlier. Instead, things had changed slowly over time, and Gerome's jealousy and possessiveness had become more and more gripping, his hold on Beau tighter. Beau realized now just how low he had sunk and what it had taken to make him see what Gerome had truly become. His left arm ached slightly at the thought.

"You had one too?" Beau asked, and Mitchell nodded. "Yeah, Gerome hit me. That was when I knew I had to get the hell out. But we were legally married, so I divorced him and left. He's an artist, and we owned the house and his studio together. When he showed up today, I told him he had to sell it, and tomorrow I'll call the attorney and get it on the market." Beau rubbed his arm without thinking about it as though he needed to soothe the aches and marks that were no longer there. He had never been so grateful for premarital agreements in his life. "He's going to have to find somewhere else to live and work, but I don't care anymore. He's had long enough, and I need to get on with our lives." He closed his eyes, bringing Jessica closer as he inhaled her light, sweet scent. "It took me three years to commit to Gerome, and I should have realized there was something wrong then. But I was a fool. This little one had my heart in her hands after, like, two days." He smiled as a timer dinged in the kitchen.

"That should be dinner. Give me a few minutes to get things ready and come on in." Mitchell hoisted himself off the sofa, lightly patting Beau's shoulder as he passed.

Beau closed his eyes. He wanted to take Mitchell's hand and hold it there just to keep the tenderness going. It had been way too long since he'd had someone, anyone, treat him gently. Gerome had at first, but things had changed over time to the point that a simple touch sent a wave of longing through him.

Chapter 3

"THE DINNER was amazing, thank you," Beau said with a satiated smile. He'd put Jessica in her carrier, and she slept through dinner, the carrier resting on a chair, with Randi on the floor nearby. Mitchell didn't want to break it to Beau, but it seemed the small dog had latched on to Jessica. When he'd left to finish dinner, Randi had stayed with Jessica on the sofa. It wasn't until Beau and Jessica came into the kitchen that Randi padded after them.

"You're welcome." Mitchell cleared the table as Jessica yawned and started making little sounds like she was waking up. By the time he was finished, Jessica was blinking up at both of them, kicking her legs. Beau played with her and got a few gummy grins. Mitchell tried playing "Where's the baby?" and got a few of his own. "Will she stay awake for long?"

Beau shrugged. "She'll be hungry in a little while, and then she'll sleep again. Sometimes she wants to be entertained, but that doesn't last very long, and then the tummy kicks in."

“I’ll stay with her if you want to make up a bottle,” Mitchell offered, lifting the carrier onto the table. Randi watched the entire time, settling back down once she was aware that Jessica wasn’t going anywhere. Goofy dog. Mitchell played with Jessica, letting her hold his finger. Just as she started getting fussy, her daddy was there with a bottle, and she sucked it down like she was starving.

“I should take her home soon, but it’s nice spending time with someone I don’t have to burp and change,” Beau said with a wink.

Mitchell didn’t want him to leave. It was pleasant having someone over for dinner. Other than the dogs, he didn’t have a lot of company out here on the farm. After things had gone south a few years ago and he had returned to the house where he grew up, Mitchell found out just who his friends were and who had been Luke’s. Not that it really mattered. Luke had been a complete ass, but he had gotten to their friends first, so they got his version of what had happened between them. Suddenly their friends were Luke’s friends, and Mitchell had found himself on the outs with just about everyone.

Jessica didn’t even finish her bottle before she fell asleep once again. Beau burped her, and she didn’t even wake up when she belched and then settled on his shoulder.

“She loves her daddy,” Mitchell said quietly. “You know, if you want to come back to the living room, I could put on a movie or something.” Maybe

Beau needed something more adult to do just as much as he needed the company.

There were times when he craved the company of other people, and then just as quickly, he pulled away from them again. He had a lingering feeling that was a final parting gift from his ex, the asshole. Mitchell was determined to try to overcome that impulse. Beau seemed like a nice man, if a little tired and pulled thin. He also had a ready smile and bright eyes that didn't have an ounce of darkness in them.

It was really funny, but he hadn't thought Luke would act that way toward him. He had always had a temper and a drive to get his own way, that was for sure. Mitchell had thought it was part of Luke's job as a financial advisor. He had to be strong and driven in order to make it in that business. But he hadn't expected that drive to manifest itself in such a controlling and then oppressive way in their relationship. Looking back, Mitchell could see the darkness in him, the way Luke shut part of himself off and tried to hide it instead of dealing with it. The Mr. Hyde part of him was always there. It just took time before it came forward, but then it had gotten really ugly.

Mitchell felt the urge to return to his dogs. They were like his relationship therapy, always giving love without fail or reservation. Maybe what he really needed was one of those dog shifters like in the Eli Easton books he liked too much.

"As long as it isn't too loud, watching a movie would be nice," Beau said, gently transferring

Jessica to her carrier. She didn't wake, and he put the carrier on the floor, Randi right next to it like a small guard dog.

"What's with her?" Beau asked.

"I think she's watching over her," Mitchell explained. "She's never been aggressive, but something about Jessica draws her. Dogs are very intuitive, and they bond sometimes with the person they want. It can be strange who they pick, because it isn't necessarily the person who feeds them." He gently stroked her head, and Randi closed her eyes, settling onto the cushion.

"Have you ever brought one of the dogs home from the shelter before? Is this something you do to give them an outing or something?" Beau asked, sitting on the side of the sofa nearest to Jessica.

"No. I don't want to give the dogs false hope. If I could, I'd probably bring all the dogs home and keep every single one. That's why I keep the dogs in the shelter and work so hard to find homes for them." There was a part of his heart that he was afraid to give away once more.

"Well, if you don't mind my saying so, I think you have someone who wormed their way into your heart." Beau smiled and even he reached over to lightly stroke Randi's head. "I'd say she's a keeper." He fiddled with the blankets. "What movies do you like?"

Mitchell brought up his cable on demand and let Beau choose one. "Would you like something to drink?"

Beau groaned. "Do I dare have a beer like an adult? It's been so long."

Mitchell brought glasses of a local microbrew from a growler and set them on the table. "It's a red ale from Molly Pitcher. I love what they do." He sat on the sofa as well.

"Is this okay?"

"*Singin' in the Rain*?" Mitchell said with a smile. He would never have guessed Beau would choose that. "I love old movies too, and Debbie Reynolds is so cute in this. Such a talent." He leaned back as the movie started. "Thank you for staying." He turned and found Beau staring back at him. Mitchell wasn't sure what the look meant for a second until a flash of hunger passed across Beau's eyes. It didn't last long before he turned back to Jessica with a sigh. Then he lifted his beer and drank a good portion of the glass.

"That is good," Beau commented, setting the glass back on the coffee table. "For a while I thought my life was going to be nothing more than diapers and bottles. Maybe it is right now. But it's nice to be able to have a few seconds where everything doesn't remind me of wipes, poop, or formula." For the first time, Mitchell saw Beau relax.

The movie continued, with Gene Kelly dropping into Debbie Reynolds's car. Beau and Mitchell finished their beers, and Mitchell brought in the last of the growler and filled up the glasses before sitting down once again.

"My mom used to love this movie," Beau said quietly, his voice filling with a loneliness that

Mitchell understood. He turned to meet his gaze, which pulled at him, wanting to draw him closer, but Mitchell resisted. Not only did he have no idea if Beau could be interested in him, but he didn't trust his own judgment where men were concerned. Not anymore. "The first time I watched it, I must have been about fourteen. Dad was working late at the office, and she and I sat on the sofa together, watching this and waiting for him to come home on a Friday night. Turned out the only work he was doing was on one of the assistants in the building. While we were waiting for him with popcorn and soda, he was getting his weekly dose of liquor, leather, and lashes. Dad apparently liked to have the women in his life paddle and use a crop. Mom divorced him when she found out about Marcy. It had apparently been going on for years and she had no idea." Color rose in Beau's cheeks and he shook his head. "I have no idea why I just told you all that. Maybe it's the baby haze and I'm still so tired I have no idea what I'm saying." He turned back to the television. "Sorry, I didn't mean to take us on a trip down dysfunctional marriage lane with a stop at S&M-ville."

Mitchell chuckled. "That's pretty funny. Not what happened, but my mind painted images of S&M-ville, with streetlights shaped like ball gags and floggers hanging from whipping posts. God, sometimes my mind takes the weirdest trips." He paused the movie since it seemed like they were going to talk for a while.

"I guess so," Beau said, chuckling along with him. "It's weird thinking of my dad… you know. I mean, I heard what he liked and all because my mom was yelling and everything, but now as an adult, I don't really want to think of my father that way."

"Do you see him a lot?" Mitchell asked.

Beau shrugged. "Rarely. He got married again and had more kids, so he's got a whole other family that I don't fit in with. But since he found out he's a grandpa, Dad has been calling more. I don't know if that means he wants to be part of our lives or if he's just enthralled with the novelty of it. Mom is thrilled and says she's going to come up for a visit. She's out in Arizona in a retirement community and loves it. What about your parents?"

Mitchell swallowed around the lump. "My folks are both gone. Dad contracted lung cancer about ten years ago and hung on a lot longer than the doctors thought he would. Mom passed four years ago of a heart attack. Apparently there had been some defect in her heart that no one knew about." He wiped his eyes. "When she died, I inherited the house here and opened the clinic in town. Mom and Dad farmed all their lives. I have about five hundred acres in total, about three acres of which are right around the house here, and the rest is leased out to a local farmer. He's growing corn right now, but next year it will be alfalfa. There are also some hay fields that one of the horse farms harvests. The rents aren't huge, but they pay the taxes on the entire property and bring in a little bit above that." Mitchell felt himself drawing inward all of a sudden. He hadn't shared this much information with someone he had just met… probably ever. Not even with his ex.

"I take it your dad was a farmer… like, full-time."

Mitchell nodded. "My dad loved the land. It was part of his soul. When he got sick, he worried so much about the crops and all the things to be done. At that time, I had my bachelor's and was starting veterinary school. Usually I worked as a veterinary assistant in the summer, but that year I came home and worked in the fields. When he was feeling okay, we worked together. There were many times when Mom climbed on the tractor and spent the day working like a trouper. This land was part of Dad's soul. So after they passed, I couldn't give it up. I thought about it. But I know every inch of this land. I swam in the creek that runs through part of it. I built a fort in one of the trees. When it came to me, I was determined to keep it, and I figured out a way to make that happen." It might not be what his dad would have chosen, but the land was being treated well. Mitchell had his animals and enough room for some more if he chose.

He restarted the movie because he needed something less emotional right now. Talking about his parents brought back all kinds of memories, some great and others nearly as black as night. Those he was going to have to deal with eventually, but he wasn't going to talk about them with Beau.

"Are you okay?" Beau asked, leaning a little closer.

Mitchell shrugged. "I'm fine." Opening those particular boxes in his head was not something to do when watching a movie with his neighbor for the first time.

They fell quiet as Gene Kelly, Donald O'Connor, and Debbie Reynolds sang and danced their way through the romantic comedy. What surprised him most about watching the movie with Beau was how comfortable he felt. They sat without talking for quite a while, and there were no uncomfortable moments, no needing to comment or fill the time with chatter. But Mitchell did find himself glancing over at Beau, especially during the funny parts, just to see him smile and watch the delight dance in his eyes.

At the grand romantic finale, Jessica began stirring, and Beau lifted her into his arms. She quieted immediately, probably just wanting her daddy. Randi bounded up off the floor and onto the sofa next to him, watching Jessica closely before settling right next to Beau's leg, her head on his thigh, looking up at both of them. Eventually Jessica began to fuss.

"What's with you, little miss?" Beau asked, getting her into the carrier. "Are you tired?"

Mitchell lifted Randi into his arms as Beau got ready to go. After turning off the television, he put Randi down and cleaned up their glasses as Beau got his things together. Mitchell was disappointed that they had to leave so soon, but he understood that Beau was on Jessica's schedule and her needs had to come first. It was just nice to have some company for a while. Randi followed Beau wherever he went.

"Thank you for a wonderful dinner and a nice evening." Beau gave him a single-arm hug, the diaper bag bouncing off Mitchell's back.

Mitchell opened the door, and Beau stepped out into the night. Mitchell made sure the outdoor lights were on as Beau headed down the driveway and turned toward home.

Randi dashed out, but Mitchell snatched her up before she could make a break for it, her little legs racing through the air. "It's okay, little girl." Randi wriggled intensely before calming, and Mitchell took her back inside. "I see you really like them." He closed the door and set her down. Randi hurried back to the door, barked twice, and then bounded up into one of the chairs, propping her front legs on the arm so she could see out. "Okay… I get it. I'm chopped liver."

Randi turned and stared at him with big eyes. She whined and turned her attention back out the window. Mitchell figured she had the right idea and peered around the curtains just as Beau and Jessica made the turn out of the driveway and down the road.

Mitchell let the curtains fall back into place and looked down at Randi, who stared back, like he was supposed to run out after them and bring Beau and Jessica back. "They'll come over again."

Randi scooted back, lowering her front paws to the cushion of the chair before curling into a ball. He could almost read her mind as she watched him.

"Yeah, I know. And yes, you can stay here with me." Mitchell had been contemplating bring Randi into the house permanently. He was surprised she hadn't been adopted out, but maybe this little one was meant for him. He left her in the living room and got two bowls, filling one with water and putting it on the floor. Then he went out into the pantry for the extra bag of food and put some in the other bowl, which he set next to the water.

Randi jumped down to explore both. She ate a little and drank before climbing back into the chair.

"You think that's yours now, huh?" Mitchell got a towel, lifted Randi, and laid the towel on the cushion. She settled once again, and Mitchell figured he might as well go to bed. He would need to be up early to care for the dogs. After checking the doors, he turned out the lights and stopped in the bathroom to clean up.

Once in his bedroom, he stripped down and climbed under the sheets he'd changed that morning. It took maybe five minutes before Randi jumped on the bed with him and curled up at the edge of the blankets. He should have known that was going to happen. Mitchell sighed, contemplating putting her back on the chair and closing his bedroom door. But it was nice having the company. The nights were usually long, dark, and lonely. Having her here might keep some of the dreams that haunted him at bay.

Mitchell sighed once again, and Randi did the same, scooting closer, like she felt his need for comfort. Heck, maybe she did. Mitchell had always thought dogs were intuitive creatures, and if that was true, then maybe her coming in was her way of providing comfort.

Yeah… right. Still, he smiled and closed his eyes, willing the nightmares to stay in their place. And they did, but it wasn't Randi that kept them at bay—it was dreams of a certain handsome neighbor.

Chapter 4

"GOOD MORNING, little girl," Beau said the following Saturday morning. "You slept good, didn't you?" He picked Jessica up and took her right to the changing table, where he got her diaper off and her little butt washed up before putting on another and dressing her for the day. Jessica tolerated him getting her into her onesie before she screwed up her little mouth for a cry of hunger of epic proportions. Beau was well aware of this fact and lifted her up, popping in the bottle he'd brought into her room with him before she could get in a really good second scream.

His phone vibrated just as he got her settled, and Beau tried to figure how he could answer it. Parents definitely needed more arms, and at the moment he was out of them, so he fed her and let the call go to voicemail.

He checked the display once she had eaten and Beau could settle her on a blanket with a play gym overhead. The number wasn't familiar, but there was a message. "This is Mitchell. I have office hours this morning, but I was wondering if you and Jessica might want to go for a walk with Randi and me this afternoon. There are some great parks."

Beau called him back as Jessica batted her favorite elephant hangy toy.

"Mitchell, it's Beau." He heard barking in the background.

"Quiet, you little beast," Mitchell said. "Randi has adopted me, and she's really excited right now."

"So she wormed her way into the house after all?"

"Yeah," Mitchell drew out. "I should have known it would happen eventually. But I really blame your daughter."

"Oh, so you getting a dog is the fault of a four-month-old," Beau quipped.

"Exactly," Mitchell deadpanned and then laughed. "Actually, she's a great companion. I need to take her for a walk this afternoon."

"Jessica and I would love to come, as long as the nice weather holds," Beau said, looking at Jessica. "Do you want to see your puppy friend?" he asked, and she kicked her feet as she batted her elephant, giving him a happy, open mouth. "I'll take that as a yes." He grinned, returning his attention to the call. "Do you want me to come pick you up? That way I won't have to move the car seat." That was a huge production.

"Perfect. If you want to come at one or so, I can pack something to eat and we can have a picnic."

"Even better. I'll see you then," Beau agreed, and they ended the call. "It looks like we're going to go out for a walk today." He grinned back at Jessica and wondered what he should wear and why he was absurdly excited. It was just a walk and some lunch in the park, but it brought a smile to his lips.

GETTING A baby ready to go anywhere took time, and this was no exception. Beau got everything together and Jessica in her car seat only to remember that he forgot the sunscreen and had to rush back inside to grab it. He got in the car and drove the short distance to Mitchell's, where he and Randi were waiting on the porch.

"I need to go inside and change her before we go," Beau explained, rolling down the window to air out the car. He climbed out, and Mitchell escorted him inside to the bathroom, where Beau changed her, and her clothes, because yes, this was one of those times. Once she was clean and dressed again, he left the bathroom. "Thank you."

"Are you ready?" Mitchell asked, holding the end of a bouncing Randi's leash. "She's been this way since you arrived."

"Good God." Beau grinned and carried Jessica back out to the car and got her in her seat. Randi jumped up next to her, tail wagging as she watched the entire process, then sniffed Jessica, licked her hand once, and settled down on the seat like she hadn't spent the past few minutes completely spazzing out. "It's pretty amazing how Randi acts around her."

Mitchell groaned. "I swear my dog loves your daughter more than anyone else."

"She doesn't act like that all the time?" Beau asked.

Mitchell shook his head. "Since I brought her into the house, the only thing she gets excited over is dinner. I swear, I came home from being gone all day, she goes out and then follows me around. There's no yipping, no running around like she's excited to see me. Your daughter comes over smelling like a stink bomb, and Randi goes berserk. Look, now she's guarding her." The little Chihuahua mix was too cute for words.

"I don't know what to say." Beau turned and shared a smile with Mitchell before starting the engine and pulling out of the drive. "Where are we going?"

"There are a couple of places, but I thought we could head south of town. It's the closest state park, and there are some great trails that are flat, so pushing the stroller won't be rough." Mitchell turned and made faces at Jessica, who seemed to giggle. It was a glorious sound as far as Beau was concerned. "You are such a pretty girl." Randi snorted. "Yeah, you too, you little beast." He turned back around and guided Beau out to the park.

"Do you come out like this often?" Beau asked.

"Sometimes. I like to bring a few of the dogs if I can so they can walk a good ways."

"Did you adopt out any more?" Beau asked.

"Yeah. I had a couple who were interested in Sweetiepie, so we'd already done the background check, but they ended up choosing Oscar instead.

Maybe it's because I want it so bad, but I keep hoping that Sweetiepie will find her forever home." He gave Beau a few more directions, which weren't too complicated, and they arrived at the state park parking area.

The day was warm, with a slight breeze and thankfully not too much humidity. Beau had been worried that Jessica would get too warm, but she seemed happy and alert as he got out the stroller and attached her carrier to the base. Beau loved the all-in-one design with the carrier fitting right into the stroller so he didn't have to get Jessica out and then into the stroller again.

"Dr. Brannigan," a young man called, hurrying toward them. He seemed in his early twenties, with a freckled face and earnest expression.

"Hi, Ryder. What a coincidence," Mitchell called with a smile that sent a stab of darkness running through Beau. His belly clenched and he wanted to growl. There was something too energetic and attentive in this young man. He didn't like the way he looked at Mitchell like he was a buffet and Ryder had his knife and fork ready for a taste. Beau fussed over Jessica, hands fumbling, to try to cover up his unrealistic jealousy. "What are you doing here? Did all the animals at the clinic get fed and looked after before you left?"

"I like to run here when I can." His expression turned more serious. "Oh yeah. They're good. Whiskers should be ready to go home, and I called her owner to pick her up tomorrow. Boxer was picked up just after you left." He rocked back and forth on his heels, he seemed so excited. "Before I go home, I'll stop in to make sure they're all settled in for the night."

"What about Blue?" Mitchell asked. "Is he still doing okay?"

Ryder swallowed. "He was napping when I left. He's breathing a lot better than he was when he came in and was up and about for a while. When I go back in, I'll text you with an update. But he was looking good." The cloud that settled over Ryder's face and the way Mitchell worried his lower lip told him it might have been touch and go for this particular pet.

"Thank you. I'll check on him on the way home as well." Mitchell clapped Ryder on the shoulder. "Now go and have some fun." He smiled, and it seemed to Beau from the way Ryder leaned forward that he wanted to ask Mitchell about joining him, but then he nodded and turned away, heading off toward the trails. "He's new at the clinic and so eager."

Beau nodded, figuring Ryder was eager for more than just work at the clinic. That young man had his eye on a particular veterinarian. Not that Beau had any right to tell Mitchell what he could and couldn't do—they had just met—but the wave of possessiveness that slammed into him took Beau by surprise. He had never felt that way about Gerome. Of course, Gerome had been possessive enough for the both of them.

Beau brought his thoughts back to Jessica and the present, still watching as Mitchell leaned forward, stretching his jeans tightly over a perfect butt while he got the leash on Randi. Damn, he was a fine-looking man. Not that it mattered, and his little bout of jealousy was useless as well. He had a daughter to take care of, and he needed to keep his attention focused where it belonged and not on some fantasy of a love life.

"Are you ready to go?" Mitchell asked. "I know this little beast is." Randi pranced around the stroller, occasionally trying to jump up into it. "Now, that's not for you," Mitchell scolded her lightly as he grabbed the basket and cooler from the trunk and they headed over to one of the green picnic tables in the shade. Randi jumped onto one of the seats, wagging her tail as Mitchell started setting things out. Beau used that time to feed Jessica, who sucked on her bottle as though she were starving before her eyelids grew heavy and she fell asleep.

"I swear that dog would climb into the carrier with her," Beau said, scooting Randi away from her to sit down. His stomach rumbled as Mitchell brought out sandwiches, fruit, and even olives and pickles for them to munch on. It was quite a feast.

"She definitely would. Randi has this fascination with your daughter." Mitchell leaned over the table. "Have you ever met a dog that was more interested in a baby than food?" He shook his head.

"What are you saying?" Beau asked as he snagged an olive and popped it into his mouth.

"That the little beast loves your daughter more than anything. Dogs bond with people, and I think she's decided that Jessica is her person." Mitchell smiled as Beau felt his eyes widen.

"Are you saying you want me to adopt Randi? I don't think I can take care of anything more right now. I'm barely holding it together sometimes just making it through the days with Jessica." Everything seemed to overwhelm him lately. More than once he had wondered if he was cut out to be a parent. Beau loved Jessica with all his heart, but he kept wondering if he was going to do something that would damage her forever or something. His attention needed to be on her and….

He took a steadying breath and held it, then released it slowly to try to calm his racing thoughts.

To his surprise, Mitchell placed his hand on his. "No. I understand. But my dog loves your daughter best." He chuckled as Randi stood, tail wagging furiously, eyes bright. She knew they were talking about her.

Beau reached over and stroked the energetic little dog's head. She soaked in the attention before turning back to where Jessica slept and settling on the bench with a soft sigh. She was a single-minded little thing. Beau broke off a small piece of bread and fed it to her. "She really is a cute little one."

"Yes, she is." Mitchell opened a container of fresh grapes and pineapple. "Let's finish up and we can go for a walk before Jessica wakes up again and needs to be fed."

Beau reached to Jessica and lightly touched her little hand. She was adorable and precious. "This little girl had my heart the very first time I saw her." He hadn't thought that was possible after the mess with Gerome, but Jessica proved that his ex hadn't killed off his ability to feel. But he wasn't sure if he was capable of loving someone the way he had Gerome. Fuck, he hated the way thoughts of him kept interrupting his everyday life. He should be able to let it go and move on. Beau pulled his thoughts back to Mitchell, trying not to let his past cloud what was turning out to be a nice day.

Mitchell leaned over the table, and Beau stiffened for a second before relaxing when he realized Mitchell was only coming closer. He needed to stop tensing whenever Mitchell moved near to him. Mitchell wasn't Gerome and wasn't going to act like him. "I can see why. She's a real cutie." He reached over to lightly caress her hand. "I remember when I was growing up, I scandalized my mother when I told her I wasn't going to get married because I didn't want to live with a girl, but that I was going to have a baby." He grinned. "I was nine and at the height of my 'girls are yucky' phase."

Beau chuckled. "What did your mom say to that?"

"She reminded me that only girls can get pregnant, and how was I going to have a baby if I didn't get married?" He laughed out loud. "I told her I was going to go to the hospital when I was older and adopt one of the babies from there. They had plenty of them, and I was sure they would give me one if I asked them." Mitchell's cheeks reddened. "I was so dumb as I kid… and completely innocent. We lived on a farm with lots of animals, so I knew where babies came from, at least baby animals, and I had pretty much figured things out when our neighbor, Mrs. Phillips, got pregnant. I think my mother was relieved when I didn't walk up to her and say that I knew how that happened." He shrugged.

Beau was intrigued. "How did you make the leap about going to the hospital to ask for a baby?" That was kind of cute, and Beau was finally able to relax and get his thoughts to settle into the here and now.

Mitchell shrugged. "Animals sometimes reject their young. I wish I knew how it happens, but it does. Sometimes it's scent—the young get marked by another and then that's the end of it. Other times it's a complete mystery. I once saw a duckling hatch and imprint on a sheep and I figured it could work the same way for humans." They shared a laugh at the example of childish innocence. Beau liked Mitchell's laugh. It was clear and deep, and the smile lines reached almost to his eyes. It was joyful and great to be around.

Beau ate the last of what he could and helped Mitchell pack up what was left. Then he attached Jessica's carrier to the stroller. After taking the basket and cooler to the car, they headed off toward one of the trails, with the shade up to keep the sun off the baby.

Randi insisted on walking next to the stroller, half prancing, tail up, head high. "That is one goofy dog," Beau observed.

"She's just happy. When I first got her, she was so miserable, hurting, and weak. It would break your heart. After I got her on the road to recovery, she kept looking for her master, but he never showed up again."

"Do you ever see him in town?" Beau asked.

"I haven't, and I hope I don't. I'd probably punch the idiot in the nose. The things people do to their pets." Mitchell clenched his fists. "Since she was injured, he wanted to put her down. Fixing her up would have cost something, and he was too cheap."

Randi must have known they were talking about her, because she jumped around Mitchell's legs, and he picked her up. She settled in his arms and kept looking at Jessica. Maybe Mitchell was right and she did like her best.

They continued walking, and every once in a while, Mitchell's hand brushed against him. Beau liked the touch and would have liked to hold hands, but he needed to keep a firm grip on the stroller. Still, it was nice to have company who didn't put a lot of demands on him.

"Out for a stroll?" a familiar voice half growled. Beau paused and turned to stare Gerome in the eye. "What are you doing here? This isn't one of your usual haunts."

"Excuse me?" Beau asked. "How would you know where I spend my time?" The implication made his blood run cold. "Are you following me?" The idea sent fear through him. Randi growled and barked sharply, snapping her jaws in Gerome's direction. "I suggest you leave."

"Because of that?" He sneered, pointing at Randi, who tried to lunge, and Mitchell almost dropped her. Gerome yanked his hand back out of her reach, and she continued snapping like she was possessed. Either that or she didn't like being in the presence of the devil incarnate.

"Leave me alone. You aren't welcome, and I'm not going to come back to you, not now or ever. I don't want to be abused and hurt again." He stared Gerome down as best he could. Part of him wanted to back down, turn tail, and get the hell away from him, but he had to be strong. Beau had allowed himself to be taken advantage of and run roughshod over, and he wasn't going to let that happen again.

"I just want to talk—"

"No!" Beau said sternly. "I have nothing to say to you, and I don't want to see you again."

"I think it's time you moved on," Mitchell said firmly. "He's said his piece, and you need to go. Beau doesn't want to see you, and he has a better life now." To punctuate what Mitchell was saying, Randi snapped at him again. "Maybe I should put her down. I can tell you, she may be small, but her teeth are sharp, and you're antagonizing her. Both Beau and I saw it." He moved closer, and Gerome backed away.

"Fine. But this isn't over," he growled and turned back away down the path.

“Jesus, was that your ex?” Mitchell asked. “What a Neanderthal.” He stared after Gerome. “Is he a complete idiot?”

“He’s possessive and he doesn’t give up what he thinks is his, and apparently that means that other people don’t get to choose anything in their lives, including who they want to be with.” Beau gripped the handle of the stroller, trying to control his anger and frustration. “I know you like me,” he said softly.

Mitchell slid a little closer. “I do. I’d like to get to know you better.” He rested his hand on Beau’s shoulder, and Beau nearly jumped away. His entire body seemed to be in Gerome mode.

“I don’t know if I can do that.” Beau lifted his gaze from Jessica. “It’s hard for me to trust anyone… like that… anymore.” He hated the fear that raced through him like the winter wind. “And I have Jessica now….” Heat rose in his cheeks. Dammit, he knew he was trying to hide, but it was all he could do. He doubted Mitchell was anything like Gerome, but seeing him had short-circuited his mind somehow, and the fear had taken over.

“Of course it is. It was hard for me for a long time.” Mitchell backed slowly away. “Do you think this is easy right now? Granted, my ex-asshole didn’t just come jumping out of the damned bushes, but he’s still with me. I feel him sometimes, like the idiot is watching me and judging everything I do the way he always did before.” Mitchell waited, and when Beau turned to him, he looked deep into his eyes. “I feel the fear and the uncertainty just as much as you do. I thought that maybe you'd understand and that we could try to help each other." He set Randi down and straightened back up.

Beau didn't know what to think, but the near panic and fear began to dissipate. How long was Gerome going to keep a hold on his life? "Maybe you're right. We can get to know each other better and see where this goes?" He steeled himself against the doubt and anxiety he felt sure were coming, but nothing materialized. Instead, he felt okay, almost happy.

Mitchell smiled as a warm breeze blew through the trees, rustling the leaves overhead, making the sunlight dance across the ground in an expression of dappled joy. "I like that idea."

Beau nodded. "But we have to go slow." He moved off to the side as a group of senior power walkers overtook them and then continued on, leaving them quickly behind. "I need the chance to figure some stuff out."

Mitchell nodded slowly. "I understand. I really do."

They started forward again. "Have you dated anyone since your ex?"

"Yeah. I tried once before. It didn't work out very well." Mitchell's steps faltered for a second and then he fell back into stride. "He was a nice guy, and I think he really liked me. His name was Howard, and he was really smart and kind of nerdy. Not that it mattered. We dated a few times, but I was scared and jumpy all the time. Things really just didn't work out, and I know it was my fault. I wasn't really ready, I guess."

"Have you seen someone… like a professional?" Beau chewed his lower lip while Jessica stretched and shifted in the stroller before settling once again. He adjusted the sun cover so she remained in the shade. He had thought that maybe he needed counseling, but he'd resisted. He had Jessica in his life, and Gerome had been staying away. But now that he'd shown up twice recently, he felt the nerves kicking up again.

"I did for a while after I got free of Luke, and we talked a lot so I could come to the realization that what happened wasn't my fault. That while Luke blamed me for everything that happened, it was his problem, and he was the one with anger management and control issues." Mitchell stopped and gently caressed Beau's arm. Beau tensed slightly and then relaxed. "No one should be hit by the ones they love, period. And what happened with Gerome wasn't your fault."

Beau nodded. "I know that. He's the one with the issue." He had told himself that over and over like a mantra. It was the only way he could get the message to sink in.

"And you stood up to him just now. You didn't freeze or hesitate—you told him no. That was pretty brave." They both came to a stop, and Mitchell gently caressed Beau's cheek.

Beau flinched. It took him a second to process that Mitchell meant it as a caring gesture. He hoped

Mitchell didn't notice, but he lowered his hand again, and color rose in Mitchell's cheeks.

"You showed a lot of courage." Mitchell's voice was tender and gentle, not at all the way Gerome acted.

"Thanks. I just want him to get the heck out of my life. He really doesn't care about me. All he wants is for me to come back so he doesn't have to move and he can still keep his studio." Beau felt his resolve kick back into place. "And it isn't going to work. I'm going to call my lawyer and get that property on the market. He can handle it for me, and while he's at it, I'll arrange to have Gerome evicted." He had been holding off on those measures because he hadn't wanted all the drama, but this had to end. Beau sped up, walking faster as energy coursed through him. "I'm tired of that idiot running my life all the damned time." He stopped a little abruptly and turned back to Mitchell. "I think I'd love to go out. Maybe I can get a babysitter."

"My receptionist, Val, does that sort of thing on the side," Mitchell offered through a huge grin.

"Perfect. Then put me in touch with her, and the two of us can go out one evening. It's been too long since I actually had a date with someone I want to spend time with. Maybe we can try for next weekend?" Look at him, making plans and charging ahead. It truly was about time that he moved forward with a part of his life that didn't include diapers and bottles. Beau continued their walk, hoping his resolve didn't crumble like sand under their feet.

Chapter 5

THEIR WALK was good. Beau had told him of his past relationship, but Mitchell hadn't realized just how raw Beau's wounds were. Mitchell was a little disappointed and pleased at the same time. His own didn't seem as fresh as Beau's. Not that he didn't understand. Mitchell had been where Beau was, and those wounds took a great deal of time and strength to heal. The guilt and the self-doubt could eat away at someone's very soul.

"How did you get past what happened to you?" Beau asked as they rode back toward the farm after feeding Jessica once more and packing everything away in the car.

"I threw myself into work. Then my parents left me the property here, and I decided to open the clinic. Suddenly I had dozens of pets that needed me each day. I also had all the property from the farm, and I knew I didn't want to work the land. I leased it out, and the shelter grew up out of my practice because I couldn't turn my back on the dogs who needed me most." He shared a quick smile with Beau as they pulled to a stop at a sign. "I guess from there I found a purpose. The dogs needed me, and they didn't judge me or look on me as damaged or anything. I was their caregiver, and they loved me no matter what." It had been a pretty incredible realization.

"I wish I could do that," Beau said.

Mitchell chuckled. "You are and you don't even know it."

Beau didn't say anything for a while. "You mean Jessica?"

Mitchell nodded as Beau continued driving. "She needs you and she loves you. Jessica will adore you unconditionally, and you'll do the same for her. The men we fell in love with should have loved us unconditionally as well."

"Yeah, well, I haven't had the best track record with unconditional love." Beau pursed his lips as though he had said enough. Randi poked her head between the seats and then jumped forward. She landed in Mitchell's lap. She sat there wagging her tail, watching Beau as he drove. The little dog seemed to realize he needed comfort and was trying to give it. Mitchell wanted to ask about the origin of his comment, but Beau had clammed up, and he didn't feel like he had the right to push. Sometimes the people who were supposed to care about you the most were the ones who ended up causing the most hurt. Instead of asking about it, Mitchell placed Randi back on the back seat, and they rode in quiet until his phone rang.

"Hey, Red, what's going on?" Red was a borough police officer, and his calls always set Mitchell on edge because he usually knew the reason for them.

"We've got a real problem and we need your help. Can you take five dogs right now? We got a domestic abuse report, and when we went it investigate…. Let's just say it's ugly—really ugly—and not just for the people." Red sounded as upset as Mitchell had ever heard him.

"What kind of dogs, and what's the situation? Big, small, am I acting as caregiver? What's the deal?" His mind was already running forward to the supplies he'd have to get together.

"There are two large dogs and three smaller ones. These conditions are so bad that there isn't going to be any question about their owner being unfit. If you can take them and get these dogs healthy, I'll work on getting a court removal order so you can find them homes." Red's voice broke, and Mitchell took a second to relay what was happening to Beau.

"Just drop me at the farm," Mitchell said.

"Are you crazy?" Beau pulled to a stop, checked the back seat, and then continued forward. "You need help," he added as Mitchell got the details from Red.

"I'll be there as soon as I can," Mitchell said and ended the call. Then he phoned his receptionist at home. "I need your help. I have to pick up some dogs. I have a friend to help, but he needs someone to sit with his daughter. She's four months old—"

Val squealed with delight. "Where do you want me? I'd love to. Should I come to your place?"

"Yes. Just get there. We'll figure everything out on the fly." His heart raced as Beau sped up. He wasn't sure Beau was up to this kind of situation. Mitchell was a little scared about what he was going to find.

"Jessica is going to sleep for a while. I can help you," Beau offered as he turned into the driveway.

Val drove in right after them and pulled up to the house. She hurried up to the car and took the startled-awake Jessica from Beau. The grandmother of three cradled her in her arms, already cooing gently as Jessica looked up at her.

"Aren't you a pretty one," she said softly, picking up the diaper bag. "Yes, you are. Sleepy too, by the looks of it." She lifted her gaze to Beau's. "Is there anything special I need to know? When did you feed her last?"

"Her name's Jessica and I fed her an hour ago. There's formula and bottles in the bag, diapers, and wipes and extra clothes if you need them." He looked stricken as he answered. Mitchell imagined it would be hard for him to be separated from Jessica.

Val smiled gently. "Don't you worry about anything. This little one and I are going to be just fine." She smiled. "Jessica and I will be perfectly all right for a few hours. You boys go ahead and rescue some dogs, and if you get the chance, make the owners pay through the nose." She turned away to head inside with the baby, with Beau staring after her as Randi followed right behind.

Beau's conflict was written all over his face. "I can go by myself," Mitchell said gently. "You go on inside and get to know Val." He could see the doubt and worry in Beau's eyes and the way he shifted his weight. "Jessica is your baby girl. I understand." He really didn't want Beau to see what he was walking into. "I'll go load the carriers the van and get going." He patted Beau's shoulder.

"But I said I'd…." Beau seemed so torn.

"It will be fine. I've done this before. I appreciate that you want to help, but you can't leave your little girl with a stranger. So meet Val and talk to her. I'll be back just as soon as I can." Mitchell hurried away. He had plenty to do.

WHAT HE'D hoped would be fast turned out to take two hours by the time he got back to the shelter, with Red behind him in his police cruiser. The van was full, and one of the dogs rode in the back seat of Red's car. Mitchell was worn out and hoped to hell he never had to see a place like that ever again.

Beau stood outside waiting for him. "What do you want me to do?"

Mitchell's eyes were still watering, and his throat hurt from swallowing bile and heartache for two hours. "Help me a minute, please." His feet were leaden as he went inside to check the isolation area, which wasn't quite big enough for the number of dogs they had. “Let’s clear this area here.” He started moving the supplies to a smaller area, stacking them on the counter in what had once been the workshop. “These dogs have to be kept away from the others while I try to help them.” Two were definitely sick; all were infested with fleas and God knew what else from sheer neglect.

Beau moved bags of dog food and other supplies after Mitchell cleared the area and packed away all the tools. Then they organized the supplies on the shelves as best they could before returning to the new isolation area. “Should I start bringing in the dogs?”

“Yes, the large ones in there, and the smaller ones in the regular isolation area.” He was going to have to walk them separately from the dogs he already had until he was sure it was safe to integrate them.

They made for an interesting parade as they brought in the dogs. Beau and Red worked to get them settled, and Mitchell checked over each of them individually, giving comfort and in some cases an antibiotic shot for eye and ear infections. They all needed care and love. One had a wound that had been neglected, which he treated. A little poodle mix was so sick, she just rested on the floor of her enclosure, breathing heavily. For her he started an IV for fluids, and Red, the huge police officer, stayed with her while Mitchell checked out the others.

“Is she going to be okay?” Red worried. He was a strong man, intimidating, with scars on his face. He could look mean, but he had a heart as big as anything. "I can ask Terry to come help if you need it."

Mitchell shook his head. "I wish I knew. I'm hoping we got to her in time." He tried not to think about that house and the fact that they had found the poodle hiding under a broken-down sofa in the living room, trapped and completely terrified. He had no idea how long the little thing had been there.

Red gently stroked her body. "If she makes it, Terry and I will adopt her." He paused in his stroking and turned away. Mitchell continued working, not wanting to let on that he'd seen the tear run down Red's cheek.

"I'm going to take her to the clinic when I'm finished with the others. Most of them just need food, water, and some care." The poodle was the worst off. Under ideal circumstances, he would have taken her right over there, but with so many other dogs to handle, he started treating her without waiting.

"I have water and food for the others. Though there's one I can't get near. He snaps whenever I approach," Beau said.

Mitchell nodded. He knew which dog that was.

"I'll stay with her," Red offered.

Mitchell approached the Doberman's enclosure. "You're fine." He put some kibble through the bars, and the dog gobbled it up, so he added some more. Then he poured water into the bowl in the corner and the dog lapped it up. It wasn't ideal, but he was most likely starving and snapping out of sheer discomfort. These dogs deserved so much better than the situation they'd found themselves in. It made Mitchell angry, and he wanted to scream. Heck, he'd felt that way for much of the afternoon, but there was nothing to be done other than to settle them in and let each dog know that they were good pups and worthy of love.

Mitchell continued feeding him, and eventually the dog lay down, so Mitchell opened the enclosure. The dog came out cautiously and allowed Mitchell to look him over. He didn't want to sedate him, but he would if necessary. "That's a good boy." He offered more food and all the water he wanted. "You've had it hard, haven't you?"

"I think they all have." Beau's voice cracked. "How can you do this all the time? I didn't go with you and I didn't see where you found them, but I want to beat the living crap out of those people." He stayed back as Mitchell let the Doberman out into one of the runs.

"This is the worst I've seen in a while." Mitchell's hand shook, and Beau hugged him tightly. Mitchell sighed and returned the comfort. God, he'd had no idea how much he needed this, and for Beau to understand and just give it was perfection.

"She ate a few bites of kibble," Red called from the other room, and then his voice came closer. "That's good, right?"

"Yes. But don't give her too much. Let her belly get used to food again. It seems she was severely dehydrated," Mitchell answered without stepping away from Beau. Damn, he was glad he wasn't alone. This whole situation was testing his ability to hold on to any sort of professional distance. In school he was taught, just like doctors, that he needed to control himself and not get emotionally involved with the animals in his care. Otherwise it would impede his ability to do his job. But this was testing his ability to maintain that control in a huge way. "I need to finish with these other dogs and then take her to the clinic, but will you stay with her? She wants that." Mitchell was glad Red had the time to comfort her.

"I will," Red said softly and left them alone again. Mitchell held Beau tightly. God, he wanted to stay this way, but there was so much to get done. He had to remind himself that he needed to take things one step at a time.

"Go back to the pups," Beau whispered. "What can I do to help?" He pulled back and smiled.

"Have you ever given a flea bath?" Mitchell asked, and Beau chuckled and shook his head. "Then come with me and I'll show you how before I leave."

"THANKS, RED," Mitchell said two hours later, once the last dog had been treated and bathed and the poodle taken to the clinic and seemed to be improving. "Come back in a few days and you can pick up your little girl." He was dirty, wet, and exhausted. All of the dogs were in their enclosures and had been walked, fed, watered, and given some attention thanks to Ryder and Beau. Mitchell was pleased as he watched Red's cruiser pull out of the drive.

"I don't think I have ever seen so many dogs in need of care and love before in my life," Beau said from behind him. "My Aunt Rhonda, Dad's sister, used to tell me stories of how she had a dog growing up and that he hated a bath. Used to fight her tooth and nail. She told me how she always ended up soaked to the skin. But these all seemed to love it and just wanted the attention." He slid his arm around Mitchell's waist. "Is this okay?"

Mitchell hummed softly. It was more than okay. Beau was reaching out to him. He knew that took some effort on Beau's part, and it was just the sort of support Mitchell needed. He didn't want to let his mind race to conclusions, but he hoped that it meant that Beau was becoming more comfortable around him. "More than." He leaned back against Beau, allowing his own jitters to fade away. Damn their exes and the impact they had left on both of them. Damn them both to hell. "These babies were all strays that were taken in. They thought they had found a forever home, but it turned out their dream was a nightmare." He tried to hold off the ache that welled inside him, and he closed his eyes, concentrating on Beau's touch. "Red told me the father died, and they were his dogs. He left everything to his son, who moved into the house. And my God, that place was a trash heap." Mitchell had tried not to think about it while he was working, but now that he had a few minutes, it all flooded back to him. "The house was toxic; it smelled like a sewer. I wore a mask and got the first few dogs out easily. They were hungry and anxious but went readily. The others I had to look for and coax out of the house. They were scared, hungry, and needed help." He thought he was going to cry. "You don't know what it's like to look under a filthy bed or a sofa and see a pair of huge pleading eyes staring back at you, a little body trembling." He inhaled deeply, and Beau held him a little tighter.

"But you got them all out, and they're going to be okay." Beau's voice broke a little.

Mitchell didn't react because he was just as overwhelmed and strong feelings had to come out no matter how much we might want to keep them bottled up. Beau's breathing grew measured and forcibly steady. Mitchell knew exactly how he felt. It wasn't a huge leap from hurt and abused animals to the residual pain and hurt of how they had been treated. It left Mitchell cold, and he expected Beau was working through his own feelings.

Maybe asking for his help wasn't the best idea. Hell, there had been times when Mitchell had his own emotions battering at his defenses—he could only imagine how Beau was feeling at this moment.

Mitchell nodded and took a measured breath of his own, hoping his voice didn't crack and give away the near flood of anger and hurt inside him. "I did, and I'm going to find them all really nice families as soon as I can. Red is getting a judge to sign off on an order so the dogs can't be returned, and charges of animal neglect and abuse are being leveled. Once that happens, I can find those babies new homes." He hoped it happened quickly so they could all move forward.

"Should we get some dinner? I can place an order and have something delivered," Beau offered.

"That would be nice," Mitchell answered, and Beau's arms slipped away. Mitchell felt the loss immediately and wanted to ask Beau to stay just a little longer, but he had no right.

"Let's get you inside so you can sit down. It's late, and the dogs are settled for the night. They need their rest, and so do you." Beau pulled the barn door closed.

Mitchell trudged toward the house. It had been a while since he'd been this tired and emotionally drained. He had been expecting a half day off and yet had worked harder than he did most full days in the clinic. Not that he regretted it for a second.

Beau took his hand, and Mitchell was so grateful for the touch and the silent support. He wondered what they could order that would be delivered out here. Pizza was an option.

Mitchell opened the door to the sweetest, most amazing scent that had ever tickled his nose. "Val…," Mitchell breathed as his appetite kicked in. God, that smelled good.

"It's just some chicken corn soup," she said softly, holding a sleeping Jessica. "This little one was a total angel. I changed and fed her half an hour ago, and she went right back to sleep." Val stayed seated with Randi right next to her, watching over the baby like she always did. "I've kept it on low heat, so you two go on in and eat." She gently passed Jessica to Beau, who practically glowed as he held his daughter. Some of the tension in his face flowed away as he cradled her, rocking gently.

"Come on." Val took command of Mitchell's kitchen and fixed them bowls of soup, along with fresh toasted bread that she must have brought with her.

"This is wonderful," Beau said as Jessica slept on. Mitchell supposed that one of the skills a parent had to master was eating one-handed. He ate as well, letting the warmth and richness of the soup soothe his jangled nerves.

"I'm glad you like it," Val said. Mitchell more than liked it—this was a bowl of heaven. "How did it go with the dogs?"

Mitchell shivered and set down his spoon. "They're all going to be okay." That was all he wanted to say right now. He had had enough of that place. Thinking about it threatened to ruin his appetite. Maybe in a few days he could tell her more, but at the moment, everything was too close to the surface. It was all he could do to keep his hands steady and not spill his food all over the table. "The one that was worst off is eating, and we were able to rehydrate her. Red is going to adopt her in a few days once she's out of isolation." That was the one bright spot of the entire ordeal. "He fell in love with her and stayed with her while she was being treated. I can help them with their wounds and get them healthy, but some of those dogs are going to carry scars on the inside for a long time."

"They'll be okay as long as they get the love they need." She smiled. "You're a good doctor and you care a great deal. But I think you need some more help. Caring for all these dogs and keeping the hours at the clinic that you do doesn't give you much time for yourself." Mitchell noticed the way her gaze shifted to Beau. "You need to be able to have something and someone for yourself." She reached across the table and gently patted each of their arms. "Let me take her while you finish eating, and then I'll head on home." Val rocked Jessica gently as she went into the other room, with Randi padding along behind.

"I think your daughter has two admirers," Mitchell teased as he took a few seconds to watch Beau. Heck, he could spend hours looking, following the contours of his neck, the wave of his hair, and the way his lips curved at the corners. Beau was something to see, and Mitchell could feast his eyes for a very long time.

"Yeah. I wish I had some of that kind of easy friend-making ability." Beau finished his soup and set down the spoon, then took a bite of his toast. "I always found it hard to make friends when I was growing up. My father…." He took another bite of toast. "My dad worked irregular hours sometimes, since he often got the shifts other employees didn't want. Dad usually did what he needed to do. He wasn't dumb, just always looking for the big score I guess, so we ended up moving when he had to get a new job every now and then. When times got tough, he was the first one they let go. I attended a number of schools and was the new kid all the time. I guess

I didn't have time to make friends before we'd have to move again."

That must have made for a very lonely life. Mitchell understood a little more about Beau now, and yeah, maybe that past had opened Beau to a guy like Gerome.

Mitchell clenched his hand under the table. What really sucked was how ever-present their exes seemed to be right now. Sometimes it felt like Luke was in the same room with him, looking over his shoulder. Just the idea gave him the creeps, and he actually turned just to make sure.

"Why didn't your dad just find a new job in the same place?" Mitchell asked.

Beau pushed back the bowl. "Because Dad always thought he was the greatest gift to any employer he worked for. When they fired him, he always decided to get even somehow, and word got around really fast. Once he tried to set the business on fire. Dad said they were wrong and that he was getting gasoline to fill up the car, but…." He sighed, and Mitchell groaned softly.

"Dad and I didn't always get along. He had his ideas, and I had mine. Pretty typical stupid kid stuff. I always thought I had better ideas than he did and wondered why Dad never listened. But I loved him, and he did his best for us." It was hard for Mitchell to comprehend the kind of childhood that Beau must have had. His dad sometimes yelled, but he was a good man overall and he provided Mitchell with a safe place to live and a good childhood. It was strange—they had fought sometimes, but now that his dad was gone, Mitchell missed him a great deal.

"Did he get to see you as a vet?"

"Yeah. He passed away a year after I graduated. I think it was the proudest I had ever seen him." There were times when he would give anything to see that expression again… to see anything of his mom and dad once more. "I miss him."

Beau shrugged. "I wish I could say the same. Mine lives a thousand miles away, and that's too danged close for me. He has a new family, but keeps trying to get in contact. The last time he visited, Dad spent the entire three days trying to convince me to put some money in this business venture he was trying to get started. I didn't, and he was none too happy about it, but he keeps trying. Dad and Gerome always got along, and I think that should have been a clue of the kind of ass my ex was." Beau cleared his throat, and Mitchell took his hand. He could understand his frustration. "It seems like my life is filled with people who only want something from me."

"I'm sorry. That must have been really difficult."

Beau nodded. "I wouldn't have any idea how a parent is supposed to act if it weren't for my grandparents. My mom is great and always did her best, but her folks were wonderful. They used to take me for a month each summer. We always had fun, and I never wanted to go back home. They had money, and my dad was always trying to get his hands on it. He would put my mother up to asking them for help all the time. But they figured it out." Beau smirked. "When they died, they left their estate in trust for me. Dad was so angry, and I think Mom was disappointed. I think they had been counting on that money, but it was tied up and they couldn't get at any of it."

"They didn't leave them anything?" Mitchell asked.

"A few thousand dollars and that was it." Beau's gaze became tougher. "That's why I need to sell that property I have with Gerome, so I can get that money back and go on with my life." He pulled his hand away and stood to take the dishes to the sink. His back was straight, his steps tight; the tension rolled off him. Mitchell wanted to ask questions, but he got the idea that Beau had said all he was going to. "I should probably take Jessica home. She's going to need to be changed and fed again soon, and then I should get her ready for bed."

Mitchell cleared the rest of the dishes before joining Beau and Val in the other room.

"Thank you for watching her," Beau was saying while he packed up the diaper bag.

Val passed the baby into his arms, and Beau put her over his shoulder and pulled out his wallet to pay her.

"Any time, young man." She took the bills and peered at the baby. "This little one is just the cutest…." She grinned and smiled at the sleeping baby before getting her purse. "I'll see you at the office."

"Thank you," Mitchell said as Val left the house. Mitchell helped Beau get his things and followed him outside. Randi tried to go along, but Mitchell kept her inside. "I'm sorry things didn't work out the way we planned them."

Beau got Jessica secured in the car seat and closed the back door. "It was a good day." He turned toward the front door, and Mitchell leaned forward and kissed him lightly. He had wanted to do that all day long, and to his delight, Beau returned his soft kiss. It sent a zing of delight running all the way through him.

Mitchell pulled back as they ended the kiss, breathless and a little dizzy. He had expected the kiss to be nice, but he hadn't counted on Beau's earthy taste and the way he made Mitchell's head spin.

Chapter 6

"GOOD NIGHT," Beau whispered. He stopped to watch Jessica sleep for a few seconds before partially closing the door. He walked quietly away from her room, and once in the living room, he checked that the baby monitor was working. He placed it next to his computer at his desk and got to work. He had hours of tasks he wanted to get done, and the best time was when Jessica was in bed.

He cleared his few emails and then set about his tasks, but his mind refused to settle. All evening, he'd thought about Mitchell's kiss, wondering what it meant. They had been close, and Beau had comforted Mitchell after he'd returned with the dogs. It wasn't as though he hadn't liked the kiss—he had. It was wonderful. That was the problem. Beau's record with relationships was complete crap, and he was still dealing with the fallout from the last one.

Beau stared at the screen and forced his mind onto the tasks at hand. He only had so much time to get things done, and he needed to focus. But as he thought about the kiss by the car, his lips tingled once again, and without thinking about it, he lightly touched them with his finger.

Okay, he was being ridiculous. Yes, Mitchell had kissed him, and he had liked it, a lot, but it didn't mean anything. Mitchell had had a really difficult afternoon and evening with the dogs, and he was probably just relieved that it was over and grateful for Beau's help.

Beau swallowed hard as his fingers hovered over the keyboard. "Come on, get your head where it belongs," he said out loud and did his best to get to work.

It took a while, but Beau was able to get his work done for the night. It was after eleven by the time he pushed his chair away from the desk and stretched his back. He was about to close his computer when an email appeared in the inbox. He narrowed his gaze slightly.

"I see you're still up," the subject read, with the body of the message blank. Beau checked the sender address but didn't recognize it. It was a Gmail address that didn't mean anything in particular.

Beau closed the message and shut down his computer before checking out the windows. Someone was watching him, and it left him feeling cold. He thought about messaging Gerome to tell him to leave him alone. This had to be part of his pressure campaign to get Beau to step back on selling the property. That was something he had no intention of doing.

Beau checked that all the doors were locked and turned out the lights, then went through the dark house one last time, checking out the windows once more. He didn't see anyone lurking near the road or on the property; no dark figure moved in the darkness. But he still felt as though Gerome was out there somewhere. Beau could practically feel his ex's eyes on him. Still, he had no intention of letting Gerome win, so he went upstairs, cleaned up, and got ready for bed. He checked that Jessica was okay and then returned to his room.

He got into bed and lay quietly, listening for any noises in the house. There was nothing. He thought about getting up to check outside once more, but he stayed where he was. If Gerome was sending him notes, then he was getting desperate. He lay there, listening and worrying, until he dozed off, only to wake with a start when he heard Jessica fussing through the baby monitor.

"It's okay, sweetheart," Beau said when he came to her. He was so tired he could barely keep his eyes open, but he changed her and carried her through the house and heated a bottle for her. He fed her as he took her back upstairs, where he sat in the rocking chair in her room, soothing her while she sucked on her bottle.

Beau wished he could soothe himself that easily.

Once she was asleep, he placed her in the crib, covered her up, and sat back in the chair. He didn't want to be alone. He pulled a blanket up over himself and rocked slowly until he fell asleep again.

Light filtered around the curtains in Jessica's room when he woke again. Jessica was still asleep, and Beau took advantage of the peace to make himself some coffee. He had just gotten downstairs when Jessica's little wails came through the baby monitor.

"I'm coming, sweetheart," Beau said and hurried upstairs. Her crying stopped as soon as she saw him.

Beau grinned and lifted her up as he spoke quietly. He had learned it didn't matter what he said—it was his tone that she responded to. "Let's get you changed, and then we can eat." He considered himself lucky that she had only been up once in the night. "I had good dreams last night." He smiled at her as he unsnapped her pajamas and then got them off. The diaper followed as she blew bubbles and chewed on her hand. "It was about Mitchell, and it was a really nice dream." He gave her little belly a raspberry and got a baby giggle in return. Then he put on a fresh diaper, followed by a onesie and light pants and a shirt. "What did you dream about? An endless stream of bottles? I bet you did." He carried her downstairs and made up a bottle just as she started to fuss again.

A knock on the door interrupted him, and Beau tensed. He gave Jessica the bottle and carried her as he went to answer the door. Beau half expected it to be Gerome with another episode of badgering, but Mitchell stood on the stoop with a smile, carrying a small box. "Good morning," Mitchell said as soon as he opened the door. "How is the prettiest little girl in town?"

"She's good, and so is her daddy. I actually slept most of the night, if a little roughly." He stepped back. "What are you doing here?" He was surprised and pleased. Beau had spent a lot of the night thinking about those dogs as well as Mitchell and how fragile he had seemed at times. He hated to leave him all alone, but with Jessica, he hadn't had much choice.

"I finished with all the dogs, and Randi wanted some exercise, so I thought I'd walk over and make you breakfast as a thank-you for all your help yesterday. I hope it's not too early. If I'm being too pushy, just say so." He paused but seemed full of jittery energy, judging by the way he shifted his weight from foot to foot. Beau wondered how much coffee he had already drunk. "I figured you wouldn't get a chance to cook for yourself very often." Mitchell's gaze raked downward, and Beau remembered he was wearing just boxers and a T-shirt. "God, I'm sorry. I guess I got the idea in my head to thank you, and I should have called." Mitchell's cheeks grew beet red. "I should go and let you wake up and…." He swallowed. "Maybe get dressed." He turned to go.

Beau's belly rumbled, and he stepped back. "It's okay. I appreciate the thought, and a home-cooked breakfast would be lovely." Part of him had wanted to let Mitchell go, but the other was flattered and thrilled that he was here. It had been a somewhat restless night, after Gerome sending that email. Probably his subconscious making the connection between him and the dogs Mitchell had rescued.

"Come on in. I need to go change. The kitchen is right through there." He pointed and carried Jessica away from the door.

"Is it okay if Randi comes in?" Mitchell asked.

"Sure." He was already heading toward his bedroom. "We'll be right back."

Mitchell snickered behind him. "Don't change on my account… please." Beau turned as Mitchell grinned. "What? The view is spectacular." Mitchell headed toward the kitchen with his box, and Beau hurried to his bedroom with Randi tagging along.

Getting dressed while holding a baby was not easy. He ended up sitting on the bed until Jessica had finished her bottle. Then he dressed and returned to the kitchen. Randi bounded around his legs, jumping up in frantic delight. The reception was nice until he remembered it was likely for Jessica. Beau buckled her in her swing with some toys, and she bounced and laughed while the kitchen filled with the scent of bacon and eggs—a simple breakfast that had his mouth watering.

"How are all the dogs?" Beau sat in one of the chairs, his attention alternating between Jessica and Mitchell. Damn, Mitchell was handsome, and more than once Beau's gaze centered on his jeans-encased butt, which sent a flash of heat running through him. Beau was glad that part of himself wasn't dead, but he wasn't sure he was ready for a physical relationship. At least not right away. Damn Gerome and his fists.

"Better than I would have thought. They're up and about. The flea baths where we could and Frontline treatments did a lot, I think. The poor things were in bad shape and so ill cared for, but they'll all be okay. Red is going to call today once the paperwork is completed. I'll feel so much better once I know they'll never go back to the person who hurt them." Mitchell checked the cupboards until he found plates, then made them up and brought the food to the table.

Beau got out some juice and glasses and sat back down, his belly rumbling. "You didn't have to do this, but I'm glad you did. I seem to only have time to reheat things for myself." He turned to Jessica. "She takes a lot of my time, and when she naps, I try to get some work done."

"I understand." Mitchell took a bite of eggs. "I need to change the subject." His smile faded from his lips. "Have you seen anyone hanging around? I swear when I was walking over here, I felt like I was being watched. I didn't see anyone. A few times Randi stopped to look around, but I get this feeling that…." His voice trailed off. "Maybe I'm being stupid. I've been thinking a lot about Luke lately, and then I feel like I'm being watched. It wigged me out a little, but then it could be my imagination."

Beau swallowed hard and jumped up. He returned with his laptop. "I got this email last night. I don't know who it's from because I don't recognize the return email address."

"So someone *is* watching?" Mitchell said, looking up from the screen. "And they're watching you, it seems." He pursed his lips, and his eyes grew stormy for a second.

Beau hated the idea. "It came to my work email address while I was up in the living room just before midnight. So it's someone who knows me, I think."

"Your ex?" Mitchell asked.

Beau sighed and forced himself to take another bite. His appetite had flown, but he didn't want to be rude to Mitchell after he'd gone to all this trouble. "That was my thought. We did see him at the park. He lives in Philadelphia, so it's safe to assume that he's either following me or hanging around to watch. The whole thing has me scared. What kind of person does something like that?" He shivered.

Mitchell got up and put his arms around him from behind.

"I mean, I know that Gerome wants to stay in his studio, but being creepy and stalkerish isn't the way to make that happen."

Mitchell leaned forward. "You know, this whole thing could be our imaginations. I know the email came in at midnight and all, but it could just be a prank. Did you see anyone around?" They both shrugged at the same time. Beau thought it was cute. "We've been talking about our pasts. Maybe we got our imaginations going overtime. As you said, if Gerome wanted something, this isn't the way to go about it. He must know that."

Beau sighed and finished eating. "You're right. I could be making a whole big thing out of a feeling." Some of the anxiety leached away. "But I'm going to keep an eye out."

"Me too."

Jessica giggled, and they both turned to where Randi was licking Jessica's toes. "Silly dog," Mitchell said and snapped his fingers. Randi turned toward the sound and then lay on the floor near the baby, watching her.

Mitchell's phone vibrated with a message, and he picked it up off the table. "Oh my."

"What is it?"

"It's from a client. Her dog was hit by a car." He stood. "I need to get to the clinic to meet them." He typed out his reply. "I'm sorry to make a mess in your kitchen and run." He picked up Randi and headed for the door. "Do you have plans for later?"

"No. I was going to spend the day here with Jessica."

Mitchell hurried back and leaned down. "Can I call you when I'm done?" Beau nodded, and Mitchell kissed him gently. "I'll talk to you then. And don't hesitate to call if anything happens." Then he was gone, taking Randi along with him.

Jessica cried, and Beau picked her up out of the swing. He checked her diaper and then just held her, rocking slightly. She calmed, and soon she was asleep on his shoulder. Beau figured he'd do the dishes later and settled on the sofa for some quiet time with his daughter. But his mind conjured up images of a little one-on-one time with Mitchell. Should he be having those kinds of thoughts while he was holding his daughter?

His phone rang, and he wriggled to get it without disturbing Jessica. He didn't recognize the number, but he answered it in case it was important.

"Mr. Pfister?" a female voice asked tentatively.

"Yes." From the tone, he expected a telemarketer, but then again, he wasn't sure, so he didn't just hang up.

She sighed. "My name is Helen van der Spoel, and I have been searching for a Beauregard Pfister. It's taken me a week to track the right person, and I hope you're him." She seemed relieved and excited. "This is going to sound a little off the cuff, but are you looking after Amy Weigl's child?"

He was instantly on his guard. "Ma'am, I don't know what this is about, but… have you been spying on me?" The past few days and the note came back to him, and a chill ran through him.

"Of course not. I've been trying to track you because you have our granddaughter." Suddenly she sounded really snooty. "My husband and I are the parents of Ronald van der Spoel, the little girl's father. That makes us her grandparents. We understand that the mother passed away, and Ronald was finally willing to give us the basic information so we could locate *our* granddaughter." The tone she used had Beau on edge. Were they going to try to take Jessica from him? Everything about the custody and placement was perfectly legal. Amy's will had been very specific.

"Ronald signed away his parental rights before Jessica was born. I have copies of the paperwork." He wanted to get her off the phone.

"Yes, we understand that. But we are still her grandparents, and we would like to see her if that's possible. You see, she is our only grandchild, and we would like to get to know her and have her in our lives." This conversation had Beau on edge.

"Ma'am, I don't know you, and while I understand that Jessica is biologically related to you, she is my daughter, and I was entrusted with her care." He intended to make his position known.

"She is still related to us by blood." Man, she was snippy all of a sudden.

"That may be." He checked his phone. "I'll have to think about it. Right now things are in a state of flux, and I'm trying to care for Jessica and get us settled in a new home." *And build a whole new life without the husband I thought I would be spending the rest of my life with, thank you very much.* "I have your number. Maybe we can arrange something." Beau just wanted to get her off the phone. He had had enough upheaval—he didn't need the sudden appearance of grandparents who were complete strangers, especially when he had no idea of their motivations. "Please let me think about it."

"We would really like to see her," she persisted. "After all, she is our granddaughter. I know our son gave up his rights, but we did no such thing." The haughtiness was almost more than he could take. "As I said, my husband and I would very much like to see Jessica."

This woman acted as though he owed her something, which got under Beau's skin something awful. As far as he was concerned, she and her husband had no rights at all, other than the privileges he might choose to give them. Jessica was his daughter now.

"It seems you've made your position clear, so now I'll do the same with mine. Jessica is my daughter, and I promised to care for her to the very best of my ability when my best friend, Amy, the one your son abandoned and wanted nothing more to do with, passed away. She knew I would care for and love her daughter… and I do. I have been a part of Jessica's life since she was born… something your son turned away from." He felt as though he needed to paint a very clear picture. "You may ask to see Jessica, but you can't demand anything. Now, I have to take care of her, and I don't have more time to talk. All I can tell you is that I will think about whether you can see her and let you know." He took a deep breath. Mrs. van der Spoel began talking again, but Beau cut her off. "Thank you for calling. I have your number, Mrs. van der Spoel."

Beau ended the call and tried to settle his thumping heart, which threatened to jump out of his chest. That was completely unexpected. He found himself wishing that Mitchell were here so he could ask him if he'd done the right thing.

HIS PHONE woke him, and his nerves jangled until he checked the display. Jessica lay sleeping on his chest. Beau answered the phone. "Hi, Mitchell. How did it go?"

The other end of the line was quiet for a few seconds. "Not so well. I had to put the dog to sleep," he answered quietly. "I hate things like that. It's always so hard." He breathed deeply. "The poor thing was deaf and didn't see very well either. The owner's husband backed out of the drive and didn't see her." He paused. "I'm…."

"Do you want to come over?" Beau thought he would offer in case Mitchell didn't want to be alone. He wasn't sure how he dealt with these sorts of things. "If you'd rather be alone, I understand." Though he needed to see Mitchell too.

"I need to check on the dogs and let them out. I'll stop by in a little while." He ended the call, and Beau slowly got Jessica off him so he could move. She woke as soon as he tried to lay her back down. She wasn't happy, and it took him some time to calm her and get her to take a bottle. By that time it was nearly his lunch hour. Fortunately he was able to buckle her into her swing so that he could get some grilled cheese sandwiches prepped and do the breakfast dishes.

It was hard not to think about Mitchell while he did mundane things. His mind had a few minutes to ruminate, and Mitchell was its favorite subject. His hands in warm water, he closed his eyes, thinking of him, the soap running through his fingers. Damn, what he wouldn't give to have Mitchell under his soapy hands, water sluicing over them as pressed his hips to Mitchell's tight butt.

A knock pulled him out of his daydream, and he yanked his hands out of the sink, spilling soapy water all down the front of him. Beau swore, and Jessica fussed as he tried to wipe off his hands and clean himself up. "I'll be right back, little girl," he said to try to calm her and hurried to the door.

Randi raced inside with Mitchell behind her. He let her off the leash, and Randi headed right for Jessica.

"What happened to you?" Mitchell's eyes grew heated, and he smiled. "Not that I'm not enjoying the impromptu wet T-shirt contest."

"Dishwashing incident." God, he hoped his cheeks didn't heat up as he recalled what he'd been thinking about. "Anyway, I have some sandwiches ready to be grilled. I just need to finish the cleanup and get out of this wet shirt." He led Mitchell back to the kitchen. Randi had her paws on the swing and was wagging her tail as she watched the baby.

"You're a good sitter, aren't you?" Mitchell said. Randi explored the room, sniffing all around, probably looking for stray bits of food. "Is there anything I can do?"

"No. I'm almost done here." He rinsed the last of the dishes and put them in the drainer, then let out the water and rinsed the sink. "Let me get out of this wet T-shirt and I'll make us some lunch." Beau hurried away and changed as quickly as he could. For some reason he didn't want to leave Mitchell alone.

"Do you want to talk about it?" He opened the pantry and pulled out a can of tomato soup. "Is this okay? I don't make it from scratch, but I do doctor it up a little."

"Of course." Mitchell seemed preoccupied. "There isn't much to say. The dog was still alive when they brought her in, but there was nothing I could do. She had so many broken ribs, and her lungs had been damaged. My only choice was to end her suffering." He placed his hands on the table. "No matter what the circumstances, I keep going over things in my head wondering what more I could have done. Ally had been a patient of mine since I first opened the clinic, and I hate to see her go."

"I know you did your best. And you said she was in pain." Beau added some milk and a few dried herbs to the soup to bump up the flavor. Then he put the saucepan on the stove to heat. "There are things that are just out of our control." God, he knew that was true. So much of his life had seemed outside of what he could influence for way too danged long.

"I know, and this was one of them for me." Mitchell folded his hands on the table. "I think what bothers me most is the guilt. Not mine, but Georgia's husband. He's going to hear that yelp and see Ally's injuries for a very long time. It wasn't his fault. Sometimes ugly things just happen. This isn't the first dog I've had to send to across the rainbow bridge, and it won't be the last." He swallowed. "At school, they told us it was part of the circle of life and that we couldn't let it get to us. But it's hard sometimes."

Jessica began to fuss, and Beau lifted her out of the swing and handed her to Mitchell. "In my experience, and it's quite limited, babies are incredibly therapeutic when we're feeling down." He smiled when Jessica settled right away, and Beau returned to finishing up their lunch. He had found that was true after the phone call from Jessica's grandmother. While he worked, he told Mitchell about the call from the rather insistent Mrs. van der Spoel.

"What are you going to do?" Mitchell asked gently. It seemed like they were both on edge.

"I don't know. I need to think about it. But my initial reaction is to tell her to pound sand. She was pushy. And yet they are Jessica's grandparents. Maybe they should see her. I don't know, but I told her I'd think about it." Part of him felt like he should play nice in case they made trouble. He just wasn't sure.

Grilled cheese and tomato soup seemed kind of plain, but growing up, it had been comfort food, which Beau needed. Mitchell seemed to enjoy it, even one-handed with Jessica on his lap. "She's probably going to want a bottle soon," Mitchell said gently as he looked into Beau's daughter's eyes. "You're adorable, aren't you?" He took a bite of his sandwich and smiled. It was good to see the gloominess retreat from his features for a little while. "Sometimes I need to remind myself that I need to look on the bright side of my job."

Beau needed that too. Jessica was certainly the remedy for a lot of life's difficult moments. He nodded as he sipped his soup. "You help animals every day, and I have no doubt that you did your best. There's nothing to feel guilty about."

"Exactly. I know that in my head, but the rest of me is taking a little longer to catch up." He ate his soup slowly, playing a little with Jessica, and gradually the mood in the room shifted.

"I've been thinking of getting a dog," Beau said. "I don't know what kind, and I want one that will be good with Jessica. But I spend a lot of time here alone with her, and I think I'd like some companionship." He looked down at Randi and smiled.

"Then why don't you keep her?" Mitchell suggested. "Randi loves Jessica and seems to like being around her. I think the three of you would be a good fit."

"She's your dog, though," Beau said.

Mitchell shook his head. "I think Randi is already Jessica's dog. She's bonded with her, and as long as she'll be loved, which I know Randi will, then she should stay here with you. That is, if you want her."

Beau grinned. "Of course I do." He reached down, and Randi came right over so he could lift her up. "Do you want to stay here with me and Jessica?" He grinned when Randi licked his face. "Kisses, huh?"

"Yup. She belongs here. Randi likes me, but I think she's taken with the two of you." Mitchell took a deep breath. "I'll bring over her things later today." It seemed as though it was a done deal, but Beau was serious—he didn't want to take Mitchell's dog.

"Are you sure? I mean she's…."

"I took her in because I liked her and she was special. Randi is adorable, but she really likes you and Jessica, and I believe that dogs pick the people they bond with. Randi obviously has an affinity for your daughter." Mitchell smiled. "She'll be happy here, and that's all I really want for any of my dogs. So please don't give it a second thought."

"You're really sure?" Beau asked, delighted. He liked the little stinker, and he knew Randi would be good with Jessica. It was a win for them, but he was still concerned about Mitchell. "You can see her whenever you like." He hugged the pup and petted her. "You're going to be happy here, I know it. We're going to need to find you a place to sleep. I'll put out some water and food for you." He was thrilled. "And you can keep me company when I have to work late." This was perfect. "Thank you."

"Don't mention it. As long as she's happy, that's all that really counts." Mitchell made for the door. "Let me go get her things so she can be comfortable. It's best if there are things she's familiar with so there's continuity." He left the house, and Beau got ready to put Jessica down for a nap. He figured he might as well let her sleep as long as she wanted.

He headed to Jessica's room and laid her in her crib. Jessica slept in her infant sack, and Randi came in and jumped into the rocking chair, making herself comfortable. Beau had little doubt that Randi was going to try to sleep in here with his daughter.

MITCHELL RETURNED with Randi's things, and Beau met him in the living room. "Where is she?"

"With Jessica," Beau chuckled. "The two of them are fast friends." He set the dishes Mitchell had brought in the corner of the kitchen. He also set Randi's bed in a corner of the living room. "Come and sit down. Can I get you anything to drink?"

Mitchell shook his head.

Mitchell really was incredibly generous, and Beau stepped closer to him. Their gazes met, the house quiet. Beau had no idea how long that would last, but he wanted to thank Mitchell for his kindness. Before he knew it, Beau was standing right in front of him, and Mitchell gathered him in his arms.

"Is this okay?" he whispered.

Beau nodded. "It's been quite a while since I've just been held."

Mitchell stilled. "Gerome never did anything like this?" His whisper was filled with surprise.

Beau shrugged. "Gerome wasn't the tender, touching kind of guy. He was more the fuck until he fell asleep kind of guy. He could go for hours, and then that was it and he'd sleep through the night, on his own side of the bed, and would complain if I woke up pressed to him because I got cold. He said he got warm, but maybe he was just stunted or something." He certainly wasn't emotionally stable, as Beau found out when Gerome's hand collided with his face. "After I left him, I got a new job and moved here. I thought I would be far enough away from him." He leaned against Mitchell, closing his eyes. "I'm sorry."

"For what?" Mitchell breathed into his ear.

"For talking about... him... at a moment like this." Beau had wanted to let go of the crap with Gerome, and yet it kept coming to mind at the worst moments.

Mitchell kissed him again, and Beau felt like he was on fire. He glanced in the direction of his bedroom and wondered if he could maneuver Mitchell that way.

"I know what you're thinking," Mitchell said, pulling away slightly. "And it's too early for that." He cocked his eyebrows. "We need to go slow."

Beau nodded as reality washed over him like a wet blanket. Hell, he wasn't even sure if he was ready for a relationship. Yes, his body was more than interested in Mitchell, and sex would be wonderful. But he wanted more than that... didn't he? Questions and caution raced through Beau's mind at the speed of light. He had a daughter now, and she needed to come first. Beau needed to care for her and make sure that she lived in a safe, nurturing environment. What if Jessica got close to Mitchell and then something happened between them? It wasn't like he could explain a breakup to a baby. He and Mitchell hadn't known each other very long, and Mitchell was right—they needed to go slow. But it was hard as well... pun intended... when his heart raced a mile a minute and with his mind awash in endorphins. "I know you're right." Beau hoped his voice didn't crack.

Mitchell stayed where he was, and Beau blinked a few times. It was difficult to clear his mind with

Mitchell right in front of him. There was something about him, something gentle and caring, thoughtful, that drew Beau. He knew Mitchell would never do the things that Gerome had done. "I don't want to go slow, though." Mitchell placed his hands on the side of Beau's cheeks, cupping his face in a gentle gesture before drawing him nearer, their lips touching softly once again. Mitchell tasted like the outdoors, fresh and light with an undertone of masculinity and spice that went right through him, all the way to his toes. Beau was drawn closer, wanting more, needing it. He steadied himself against Mitchell's firm shoulders. Mitchell's hands slid off his cheeks and down his shoulders as they came closer, their kiss intensifying as Mitchell held him tightly.

A whimper came through the baby monitor, and Beau stilled, listening for more. He'd hoped she'd sleep longer.

"Maybe she'll go back to sleep," Mitchell said as he pulled away.

"Sometimes she does, but not for very long." Beau hated to leave, but he knew his daughter. She might rest for another fifteen minutes, but….

The screech through the monitor told him that wasn't the case this time. Randi barked, and Jessica cried louder. It seemed the two of them were intent on bringing the house down.

Mitchell stared at him and then started laughing. "Dang…." He continued chuckling. "Do you want me to get her?"

Beau was already on his way. “There’s a bottle made up in the refrigerator. Can you warm it in some hot water, and I’ll get Her Highness?” He went to his daughter, who stopped crying but sniffled as he picked her up. “No one forgot you.” Beau groaned and put her on the changing table. No wonder she woke up. Her little diaper was full. He cleaned and changed her, then led the way out to the kitchen with Randi right behind. It really did seem like Jessica was going to have a little puppy shadow.

“Here’s the bottle. It isn’t too hot.” Mitchell handed it to him. Beau checked it out of habit before shaking it and placing it into her mouth. Jessica sucked right away, drinking hard, her eyes wide and watching him. Beau loved that undivided attention, like he was the most important person in the world. And maybe he was. Beau was her sole means of support and survival.

“I think I should let you do what you need to.” Mitchell shifted his weight from foot to foot. “You have enough to do without me hanging around all day. There’s some food and water out for Randi. She just needs a half cup twice a day and an occasional treat. If you give her more, she’ll eat too much and get overweight.”

“You don’t have to go,” Beau said, not really wanting to be alone. “I know I’m not the greatest company sometimes.” He didn’t know what to say. A guy with a baby had to be a bit of a letdown for an active guy like Mitchell. Beau was a basically a stay-at-home kind of guy. The college allowed him to work from home because of the baby and because he was danged good at his job. They wanted the remote learning active and robust, and they were willing to work with him to get it. He also had a baby, and that meant staying with her almost all the time. Their picnic and hike in the park had been a special outing and something rather rare for him. Things hadn't always been that way, but Jessica had brought a number of changes into his life.

"You're great company," Mitchell said, coming closer. "But I'm going to need to see to the dogs and make sure they're all fed and walked. That can take a while." He smiled and leaned over him.

Beau closed the distance between them to take a kiss. Then Mitchell was gone, and as soon as the door closed and the silence in the house surrounded him, Beau sighed and turned his attention to Jessica to keep the threat of loneliness at bay.

Chapter 7

"DR. BRANNIGAN?" his assistant, Bonnie, said as he handed a pissed-off cat back to her owner. Clyde hated shots. Mitchell had been lucky to escape his wrath—this time.

"He's going to be fine," he told Clyde's owner, who immediately soothed him. Clyde glared at Mitchell with narrowed eyes as though he were the cat devil himself.

"Thank you," Clare said and left the office with Clyde. Mitchell was always glad to see the back of that particular cat.

"Yes, Bonnie?" He washed his hands as he waited for her to talk.

"There's a man out front with a baby and a Chihuahua mix. He doesn't have an appointment, but he says that his dog has been throwing up a lot. The poor guy looks like he's going to fly to pieces at any second."

Mitchell nodded. "I'll come out to see him." He followed Bonnie into the reception area, where Beau sat with Jessica on his lap and Randi in a carrier. "What's going on?"

"I don't know. She was doing okay and then started throwing up and getting really sick." Beau looked pale and about to be sick himself. "I'm sorry if I hurt her. I was being careful and fed her like you told me. It's only been three days and already I did this." He seemed shaky and about to lose it completely.

Mitchell lifted the carrier and peered inside. "Let me take a look at her." He led them through to the examination room and put the carrier on the table. He opened it and gently brought Randi out. He held her up, and Randi's little legs shook. "What has she eaten?" He took her temperature and checked her mouth and feet for injuries or infection, but saw nothing.

"I've given her a half cup of the food you left twice a day. I haven't shared table scraps, and I don't have anything in the house that should hurt her. The place is baby-proofed already, and the cupboards with soaps and stuff are locked." Beau seemed pale and half scared. Jessica was fussy and kept squirming and whining. She knew something wasn't right.

"Has she been outside when you weren't there?" Mitchell asked as Randi coughed and brought up some more of what was in her belly. Mitchell collected it and looked it over closely.

Bonnie came into the room. "What can I do to help?" That lady always knew when she was needed. Mitchell swore she had a sixth sense.

"We need to get an IV started. She needs fluids. I think she's eaten something she shouldn't have." Randi retched again, but nothing came up this time. Mitchell hoped her belly was empty now and whatever was hurting her was out. Bonnie got the fluids ready, and Mitchell soothed Randi to keep her calm. Then he shaved a spot on her leg and got the fluids going. The poor little thing looked so helpless.

"What did I do?" Beau asked, his voice breaking.

"I don't think you did anything." Mitchell petted Randi as she lifted her head weakly. "I'm not sure what happened yet." Bonnie stayed with her and kept her quiet while Mitchell left the room. He had to review what Randi had brought up. It wasn't his favorite thing to do, but sometimes you needed to follow the clues. And he had nothing to work with… until he spied a few small grains. He separated them and looked more closely at them. Mitchell sighed as he saw what he had been afraid of. He returned to where Randi lay on the counter. Bonnie had covered her, and she was no longer shaking.

"What is it?"

Mitchell swallowed hard. "I think she ate something poisonous. I found granules in what was in her belly, and she's acting exactly like I would expect. It looks like mouse bait or something."

Beau's mouth fell open and he gasped. "You think someone did this on purpose?" He stood with Jessica on his shoulder, pacing the small room. "I swear I'll kill 'em." He clenched his teeth.

"I don't think she got very much. I'm hopeful that you got her here in time and that her own body's defenses took over. She was sick because she needed to expel what was hurting her." Randi had stopped heaving and lay quietly while the fluids slowly dripped into her.

"What can you do? Is there some kind of antidote?" Beau asked, clearly distressed.

Mitchell badly wanted to comfort him, but this was his place of business and he needed to be professional.

"Do you want me to stay with her for now?" Bonnie asked.

Mitchell nodded. "Please." Then he turned back to Beau. "I want to keep her here for a while so we can monitor her, and I'm hoping we can flush the toxins out of her system. Bonnie will put her in a quiet recovery area and stay with her. Randi isn't going to be alone. Why don't you take Jessica to the house, and I'll stop by on my way home and let you know what's going on." The thought that someone could hurt this sweet dog made his blood boil, but he had to keep calm for himself and Beau. On the inside, he wanted to find whoever had done this and rip his nuts off. Hopefully her little system was working enough that they could get the toxins out of her without them doing too much damage. Unfortunately, he couldn't do much other than keep her comfortable and hope. "You might want to check around where Randi might have gotten to see if you can find anything. Once we get her better, you don't want her to get into anything again. If you find something, call us so we will know more about what we're dealing with." He was pretty sure someone had put some sort of mouse pellets near the house. From the look of it, maybe Randi hadn't eaten it directly but had gotten it on her coat or paws and then licked it off.

"I'll do my best," Beau said.

Mitchell drew closer. "I know you will, and I'll stop at your house in a few hours to help you look." Mitchell wanted to kiss him. The sadness in Beau's eyes and the way his shoulders slumped made him want to comfort him and try to take away the pain. Granted, he knew he couldn't right then.

Beau nodded. "I'd better go. Call me just to tell me how she is." He swallowed hard, and Mitchell's breath hitched. Then Beau opened the door and left the room.

"Doc…," Bonnie said as her head appeared in the back doorway. "Are you seeing him? He's definitely a looker, that's for sure. If I were ten years younger and he were ten years older, I'd be on him like a duck on a June bug."

Mitchell couldn't help smiling, because, yeah, Beau was gorgeous. He lifted his gaze as the smile faded. "I don't know if I can do it, though." Bonnie was aware of his past. She was the only one in the office who was. She had been with him since they opened, and he trusted his secrets with her. Bonnie's mouth was like a lockbox, and he loved that about her. "I want to. It's been a long time. But sometimes when I'm with him, it's like Luke is in the room with us."

Bonnie stepped back to where Randi was. "Beau isn't Luke." Her voice drifted in from where she sat with Randi. Mitchell peered into the room. She had Randi lying on the counter, the IV still running into her. Randi's eyes half drooped, but when she saw him, she wagged her tail and tried to get up.

"Just stay there, sweetheart," he said gently, and Bonnie petted down her side.

"Luke was an ass and you know it." She rolled her eyes. "He didn't even like dogs, for Christ's sake." She glared as though that trait made him the spawn of Satan. Maybe it did. Mitchell certainly should have known there was something wrong with him right there. "And you saw Beau when he brought in this little girl. He was heartbroken that she was sick and hurting and afraid he might have done something to her. That's doggie love, and a man who can love a dog like that is certainly worth your time."

Mitchell patted the doorframe nervously. "He has had someone in his life like Luke."

Bonnie gasped. "That adorable father had someone who…?" Her lips straightened and her eyes hardened to stone. "The bastard… they both were." She lowered her gaze to Randi. "Those men who hurt you took something away. Your safety, your confidence, and the ability to trust that someone else isn't going to treat you the same way. They're thieves, and they steal other people's lives."

Mitchell found himself nodding slowly. "How did you get so smart?"

Bonnie hesitated, and Mitchell got the feeling that she was debating something. Her expression revealed nothing, which told him something was up. Bonnie was usually very expressive. "You don't think you and Beau are the only ones? My first husband was really good with his hands… until he wasn't. Then things got bad. I divorced him, but he left scars that no one could see. And I think that's how it is with you and Beau. Maybe there are physical marks, but those heal. The others stay with you longer." She left her right hand lying still on Randi's side like she needed a link to her gentleness. "The thing you have to decide, and this is the really hard part, or at least it was for me…." She paused and blinked, wiping her eyes on a tissue. "I don't normally talk about this part of my life because it still hurts. But that's the point, I guess. I decided that I wanted Marty more than the fear. That he was important enough to me to not let the hurt get the better of me. It took some time, and if Beau's hurt is fresh, then you'll need to give him that time." She turned away, and Mitchell figured her episode of story time was over.

"I know you're right. But I'm still afraid for myself, for him. What if Beau isn't ready? He's still trying to separate himself from his ex. They have divorced, but they still have property together that they need to sell, and the guy is a real piece of work."

"Are you afraid he'll go back to him?" Bonnie asked.

Mitchell shook his head. That was the least of his concerns. "I left Luke a while ago and I've had years to try to process what he did to me. Yet I'm still worried and hesitant. What if Beau…? He isn't in the same place."

"Then maybe you need to help him get there. Take your time." She rolled her eyes. "You young people like to hurry into everything. Jump each other and right into bed. There's something to be said for being courted, for someone taking their time to get to know you… and maybe even falling in love before jumping into bed. I ran after my first husband and look what happened. It was fast and all high emotion. But it didn't last, and he made my life sheer hell. Deep love, the kind that spans decades, takes time. At least that's my opinion." She patted his shoulder as Randi wagged her tail. "I think this little one is feeling better." Mitchell agreed, but only time was going to tell for sure. "You have another appointment in five minutes. I'll get her settled and ensure she doesn't pull out the IV."

"Thanks. I could sedate her, but I don't want to slow down her systems. Randi seems to have gotten rid of the bad stuff largely on her own, and the faster her little body flushes the rest of it out, the better." He needed to get back to work, and Bonnie had given him plenty to think about. Mitchell just needed to figure out what he wanted and hope that Beau wanted the same thing.

AT THE end of the day, Mitchell closed up the clinic. Randi was on the mend, but he thought it best to keep her overnight. Bonnie was scheduled to stop in and check on their patients, so he had the evening off, though he figured he would check on the little girl later as well. He hurried back to the house just as Jeremy pulled the barn door closed. "I got them all walked and fed, using the sheet you left," he said with a grin. Jeremy was the neighbor's son and he loved animals. He was fifteen but very conscientious, and he came in three days a week to help walk and feed the dogs. "I didn't walk the one you marked to stay away from. I did feed him, though."

"Great." He hadn't wanted Jeremy to try to walk the strong pit bull. He had a tendency to be stubborn, and he'd pull Jeremy where he wanted to go and could hurt him. "Thank you."

Jeremy rocked on his heels. "Mom says that now that I have a job, I can get a dog of my own." That had been an uphill battle for him for months. Apparently Jeremy's mother hadn't been convinced that her son would care for his own dog, but it seemed caring for fifteen of them sometimes had convinced her.

"You talk to your mom about the dog you want and have her call me. We can make that happen." Jeremy reminded Mitchell so much of himself when he was his age. Jeremy said he wanted to be a vet like Mitchell and had asked him a million questions over the months. Mitchell had done his best to encourage him and told him the kinds of classes he needed to take in school in order to help prepare.

"I will. I know just which one I want. The terrier, Scamper. He's great and not too big. I think a large dog will scare Mom, but he's not too old and he likes me." Jeremy practically jumped out of his skin, he was so excited. "I'll tell Mom and have her call."

"You do that." Mitchell patted his shoulder, and Jeremy jumped onto his old red ten-speed and pedaled down the drive and out onto the side of the road.

Mitchell waited until he was gone before opening the barn door. He stepped inside, and the dogs greeted him with yips, barks, and wagging tails. "I know, Jeremy was here and you're all excited." When Mitchell got to work, they settled down.

Mitchell put some of the larger dogs into the runs, including the pit bull, whose attitude and demeanor had shifted a little. He knew the strong-willed, muscular dog was going to be hard to find a home for, but Mitchell was determined to try. After checking on everyone, he left the shelter and walked across the yard.

About halfway to the door, he stopped, the hair in the back of his neck standing up. Mitchell checked around him but didn't see anyone. Still, he couldn't shake the feeling that he was being watched. He hurried toward the house and went right inside. He missed having Randi in the house. But the little dog would be happier with Beau and Jessica. Speaking of the little stinker, he called the clinic and left a message for Bonnie to let him know how she was doing when she came in that evening. Mitchell had already sent Beau a message to tell him that she had been better when he left the clinic but that she wouldn't truly be out of the woods until the morning. By then, he hoped her appetite would be back.

He went to the kitchen and made a sandwich for dinner and was just finishing when the phone rang. It was the clinic. His breath caught as he answered. "This is Mitchell."

"Doctor, it's Bonnie. I just got here, and Randi…." He stilled, bracing for bad news. "She's up and about, and I gave her a little water." She sounded happy. "That's a good sign, isn't it?"

Mitchell breathed deeply. "Yes. That's really great. Is the IV done?"

"Yes. I was about to take it out and get her settled for the night."

He smiled. "That's great. Remove the IV and give her some water and we'll give her some food in the morning. We need to give her belly a chance to settle, but this is very good news. Keep her calm and get her to rest as best you can. That's the best thing for her." He ended the call and made one to Beau.

"How is Randi?" Beau asked without any lead-in.

"Much better. She's up and drinking. We'll get her to rest, and you can come get her in the morning. Did you find what she might have gotten into?" He wondered if Beau wanted him to come down, but he didn't want to ask. Maybe Beau needed some space. Mitchell didn't want to crowd him.

"I might have. But I'm not sure." He seemed so tentative. "Can you come look?"

"I'll be right there." He hung up and left the house, looking around again as he got into the car, trying to shake that feeling that someone was there. He thought about calling the police, but what was he going to say? That he had this feeling? It sounded dumb when he ran it through his head, never mind saying it out loud.

The drive to Beau's took a few minutes, and Beau met him outside with Jessica sleeping on his shoulder. "What do you have?" he whispered.

"It looks like something was scattered over here beside the back door. But it's hard to tell." Beau pointed, and Mitchell bent down to take a closer took. Sure enough, it seemed that something that was most likely rat poison had been spread on the dirt.

"What the hell?" He glanced up at Beau. "You didn't have anything like this in your trash, did you?" Mitchell gathered a few of the stray granules.

"No. Of course not," Beau snapped. "How can you ask that? I would never poison Randi."

Mitchell stood. "I didn't mean it that way. Of course you wouldn't." Beau was upset, but Mitchell hadn't meant to accuse him of anything. "I just wanted to make sure that you hadn't thrown something in the trash that might have gotten on the ground."

Beau shook his head hard. "I don't even have that in the house." His eyes grew huge and he gasped quietly. "Then where did it come from?" Anger gripped him and Beau clenched his fist. "You don't think…?"

Mitchell wished he had some answers. “I don’t know. It would be a really cruel thing to do to try to hurt Randi. Would Gerome do that, do you think? Is that something he’d be capable of? Is there someone else who might want to hurt you?” He drew closer, brushing off his hands.

“I don’t know. I wouldn’t have thought Gerome would do half the things he did, but trying to hurt a dog? That’s pretty twisted.” He began to shake, and Jessica whimpered.

“Go on inside and take care of her. Do you have a push broom? I can clear this away and wash down the area so Randi doesn’t get into any of it again.”

“In the shed over there,” Beau answered, still shaken up. “Thank you.” He went inside, and Mitchell went to get the shovel.

The shed was small and filled with stuff that had probably been left by the previous owners. Mitchell didn’t see Beau bringing all this crap with him when he moved. Most of it was halfway to garbage, with five-gallon buckets of what seemed to be lamp parts and bits of metal. He stepped around them to get to the shovel, careful not to brush against the old tool bench against the side wall. Still, he managed to push over an old folding chair before he reached the shovel at the back. He grabbed it and turned to leave, but he knocked a paper bag off the tool bench. It fell to the floor, granules spilling out onto the wood.

Mitchell paused and bent to look closer. He picked up a few granules and ran them through his fingers. “Damn….” The air cooled instantly around him as his thoughts ran a million miles an hour. He wondered how long this had been here. The bag itself looked fresh and not too old. It wasn't crinkled all over and was still a deeper brown. He wondered if someone had brought this stuff or if it had been here. Whatever the answer, someone had either brought or found this in the shed and spread some of it around the side of the house. He had hoped his suspicions were wrong, but it seemed that someone had indeed spread the poison for Randi to find. That was the height of cruel. Mitchell's belly clenched as old memories he'd thought he'd buried surged to the surface.

Pushing the hurt aside, he grabbed the shovel and got out of the shed, then closed and latched the door. Mitchell cleaned up the area near the house, removing all of the pellets he could see, and then grabbed the hose and washed the area down well. He made sure he saw nothing more before giving the area a second hosing down. Hopefully that would clean up the mess. Mitchell then returned the shovel to the shed and swept up the spilled poison. He brought the bag in with him.

He was nervous about telling Beau what he'd found, but he knew he had to. It was upsetting for him, and Mitchell could just imagine how Beau was going to feel. He already blamed himself for what happened to Randi, but Mitchell was becoming more and more convinced that someone else was behind what had happened. "It's all cleaned up," he said when he came in through the back door.

"Thank you." Beau came in without Jessica, and Mitchell heard her in her swing. She sure loved that thing. "What's that?"

"I found it in the shed." He showed it to Beau, who paled.

"I never saw that before."

"I believe you. The bag was on the workbench." He wadded it up, and Beau handed him a few plastic bags. Mitchell double encased it and placed the poison deep in the trash and closed the child-locked cupboard under the sink. "I'll take the whole thing with me when I go and put it in the medical waste container at the clinic."

"But how did it get there?" Beau asked. Mitchell had an idea that Beau already knew the answer to that question. "God." He pulled out one of the scuffed wooden kitchen chairs and sank into it. "I don't want to believe that Gerome…."

"I think someone has been using your shed to watch things. That would explain the email and the feeling of being watched." Though it didn't account for the fact that Mitchell had felt the same way at his place. Maybe he needed to search for a hiding place on his property. If someone wanted to poison dogs, Mitchell had plenty of them. Someone could cause a great deal of hurt if they wanted to.

"Jesus…." Beau rocked slightly, and Mitchell sat in the nearest chair, taking Beau's hand.

"You had nothing to do with what happened to Randi. Someone put that stuff out there on purpose. Otherwise it couldn't have gotten there from the shed, and I don't think it had been there long." He gently stroked the back of Beau's hands with his thumbs. "She's going to be okay, and she'll be really happy to be home. For a while I'd suggest you stay with her while she's outside if you can. I washed down the area, and if there's any more, a good rain should take care of it. But until then…."

"Okay, I understand," he said absently as though he were in shock. "I can't believe something like this is happening." He scratched his head and then lowered his hands to the table, wringing them slowly. "I mean… I keep hoping that this is some accident, but I don't know how it can be." He lifted his gaze, which was filled with hurt. "I think I should call the police… but what am I going to tell them? That we already cleaned up and destroyed any evidence that we might have had?"

"Shit," Mitchell swore. "I should have thought of that." His thoughts had been on trying to protect Randi from getting into the poison again, but instead he might have messed up finding the person who was behind this. "I think I'm going to call Red anyway. At least let him know what's going on and what we suspect." There certainly wasn't any harm in it.

"Yeah, I think I'd feel better," Beau agreed, and Mitchell made the call and explained what had happened and what they'd found.

"I know we probably already contaminated the area when we tried to clean it up. But we couldn't take any chances."

"All right," Red said soothingly. "And you're sure that Beau didn't have anything like that in the house?"

Mitchell turned to Beau, relaying the question. Beau shook his head. "I've brought as little dangerous stuff into the house as I can because of Jessica. I never had any rat poison or mouse bait stuff. As far as I know, there hasn't been any need for it."

"Did you hear him?" Mitchell asked Red, his nerves jangling more and more. He needed to calm down and get his mind into gear. He wasn't going to be able to help anyone if he was a twitchy mess.

"There are a couple of possibilities that I can think of. The first is that it was some sort of accident. I don't think that's likely, though, given what you described. I doubt I'm going to get much evidence off the ground or the bag since they were disturbed. My best advice is to keep your eyes open and watch for anything or anyone suspicious."

"Okay. We can do that." They already were anyway.

"Does either of you know anyone who might have done this?" Red asked.

Mitchell explained about Beau's ex-husband and what he wanted from Beau. Red agreed that he needed to be looked into. "Anger and hurt are strong and sometimes irrational motivators." That matched with what Mitchell thought. "Unfortunately, I don't have something concrete to tell you other than to keep on the lookout and call me or the sheriff's department right away if anything happens. Be sure to explain that you have been in contact with me, and that way I can be brought in to try to help."

"Thanks," Mitchell said. He hadn't expected Red to be able to tell them much more than that, but he was grateful for his advice. At least Red didn't get angry with them for what they had already done. "I appreciate the help."

"Any time." Red hung up, and Mitchell put his phone back in his pocket.

"I wish I had thought this through before messing things up."

"It's okay." Beau sighed, and Mitchell knew he was feeling pretty low. Heck, he was too, and to top things off, their ray of energetic sunshine wasn't there. "Can we at least see if she's all right?" Beau asked.

Mitchell nodded. "Sure. If you want to get Jessica ready, we can go down to the clinic." Maybe seeing that Randi was doing better would help both of them. Mitchell felt bad about cleaning things up and not even thinking of calling the police first. But he knew Beau felt worse about Randi getting sick.

It took a while to get Jessica ready and into the car. Beau drove down to the clinic and parked in front. The parking area was empty, so Bonnie must have already gone for the night. Mitchell got out, unlocked the door, and waited for Beau and Jessica. Once inside, he left them in the reception area and quietly went in back.

Sometimes the effect of poisons was delayed and animals got better initially only to take a turn for the worse. He hadn't thought that was the case with Randi and was relieved to find the little girl standing up in her cage, wagging her tail, as he came inside. Part of her leg was bald from where he had had to shave her for the IV, but otherwise she seemed in good shape. "Sweetheart," he said softly and opened the door. He lifted her out and carried her to where Beau sat bouncing his leg.

Randi barked happily when she saw Jessica. Mitchell set her down, and she hurried over and pranced around Beau's legs until he reached down to pet her. "Is she really going to be okay?"

"Yes. She should be fine." Mitchell grinned as Beau lifted her up and hugged her gently. When she kissed his cheek, he closed his eyes.

"I'm going to be more careful, I promise," he said softly. "But you scared the life out of me, little one." Randi soaked up the attention, and when Beau set her on his lap, she settled right there, curling up into a ball. The tension released from Beau's shoulders and he actually smiled. "I'm so sorry."

"It wasn't your fault," Mitchell told him. He was convinced that someone had spread the rat poison on purpose, and he was determined to find out who and why. He had felt someone watching him, and Beau had said the same. It was pretty obvious to him that the shed had been the lookout post at Beau's. He needed to check his own property for the same kind of thing. But what baffled him was why both of them had developed a stalker at the same damned time. He and Beau hadn't known each other for very long, and other than a few outings, they hadn't spent that much time together outside their homes.

"I keep thinking it is. I should have been more careful and watchful. Having a dog is a real responsibility, and I let her down." Randi nudged Beau's hand when he stopped petting her.

"I think you're forgiven," he said gently, and they shared a smile. Mitchell drew closer and knelt near Beau and Randi. He gently cupped Beau's cheeks in his hands, waiting to see if Beau pulled away. He didn't, and Mitchell closed the distance between them. The kiss started gently, but then Beau pressed closer, his lips firm and warm. Mitchell pulled back, not wanting to push in case Beau wasn't ready for more. "Was that okay?"

Beau nodded slowly. "It was so much more than okay." He placed his hands on Mitchell's arms and rested them there. "I've been so unsure of myself when it comes to you and being with anyone again."

"I know, and I understand. It took me a long time before I could be close to anyone." Mitchell closed his eyes for a few seconds to be alone with his own thoughts, but forced himself to open them again. "It's time for me to try again. I know that it can be hard to trust after being hurt." He slid his hands away from Beau's cheeks. "But I want you to know that I won't purposely hurt you." He swallowed hard as his heart raced. Beau looked amazing, even when he bit his lower lip a little nervously, and Mitchell inhaled deeply, Beau's scent setting his head on fire. Something about Beau got his engine revving. He was hot, that was for sure, but there was something else, something more visceral. Maybe it was that Beau was a wonderful, incredibly caring guy. Dogs knew a good heart, and Beau definitely had one of those. But he also knew and understood what Mitchell had been through, and Mitchell understood some of what Beau was feeling. Not that everyone was the same and dealt with hurt the same way, but Mitchell understood the lump that could form in a person's belly just because of the way something smelled or a sound in the background that connected with a memory he hadn't really paid attention to until something clicked. Even the near panic that could come from nowhere because of what someone said at a party or something.

To Mitchell's surprise, Beau initiated the next kiss. Mitchell was really into it, especially the way Beau sucked on his upper lip.

"I'm sorry," Bonnie stammered.

Mitchell tried to back away, got his feet tangled, and ended up on the floor flat on his back. He stared up at the ceiling as Bonnie snickered at him.

"I forgot something when I was here earlier." She hurried to the counter as Mitchell did his best to get up without looking like a complete idiot. Hell, it was too late for that. "I'll be on my way, and you boys can get back to what you were doing." She hurried to the front door. "Though I'd think you could find a better place for it." The front door closed behind her, and Mitchell wished a hole would open up under him and suck him down.

"She's something else," Beau said as Mitchell finally managed to get off the floor. Randi blinked at him from Beau's lap like he was crazy. You knew it was bad when a dog thought you were nuts. "Are you all right?"

Mitchell got his balance again. "I'm fine. I wasn't expecting someone to come in, and I didn't hear her." Maybe he'd discovered a deficiency in his mind or something. When he was kissing, his ears shut off. Now that was ridiculous. "Though I should probably shower. This is the floor of a vet's office, and we all know what ends up down there." Accidents went with the territory, though they always cleaned and disinfected afterward. Still, it wasn't like he should be rolling around on the floor.

"Can we take Randi?" Beau asked, stroking her gently.

"If you like. I'd feel better if I were able to watch her overnight, though." Maybe he was being overly cautious, but he'd hate for anything to happen to the little one.

"Okay." Beau sighed rather loudly. "Look, you're probably going to think I'm crazy, but I don't want to be alone. If someone did try to poison my dog and if they've been watching me, then I don't think it's a good idea to be on my own. What if someone tried to hurt Jessica?" The color drained from Beau's face.

"You can come to the house if you like. I have a guest room, and Randi can stay with us. I can watch her and check on the shelter before bed. There's a place for Jessica too." He hadn't wanted to go pressing the panic button, but Mitchell hadn't wanted to be alone either. With all of them in the house, at least he and Beau could look out for each other until they figured out what the hell was going on. "We'll need to stop back at your place to get you some things, and then you can spend the night at my house." This seemed like the best arrangement, and it would give him a chance to check over his property too.

IT TOOK a while for Beau and Jessica to decamp at their place and haul things over. Mitchell had no idea just how much stuff it took for a baby to spend the night. There was a portable crib and stuff for feeding, toys, and enough diapers for an army. Though he found out that was an exaggeration, given the unpredictability, it was best to be prepared.

"I thought we could set Jessica up in the guest room. That way you can be close to her." Mitchell set down Randi's carrier and opened it. She climbed out and began exploring. She really was acting like the little dog Mitchell knew.

"That would be nice." Beau set down the armload of things he'd brought in and returned to get Jessica, who had fallen asleep in her carrier. Mitchell took the portacrib to the bedroom and set it at the base of the bed. He didn't try to set it up. Beau would have to do that.

When Beau brought in Sleeping Beauty, he placed her carrier well back on the floor beside the sofa and finished getting things organized. Randi took her place next to Jessica, watching her, wagging her tail for a few minutes before settling down next to her.

"Do you need any help?" Mitchell whispered.

"I'm almost done," Beau answered from the guest room.

"Okay. I'm going to check on the pack. I put the remote for the television on the coffee table if you want to watch anything. I want to let some of the dogs out and get them all settled before I close everything up for the night." He also intended to snoop around on his own property, but he didn't want to worry Beau. "I should be back in an hour."

"Okay. I can order some dinner. The brew pub does delivery. It's the least I can do. I could sure use a beer right now." Beau seemed stressed and pulled thin. Mitchell thanked him and locked the door on his way out to the barn.

The dogs seemed more frantic than usual. He put as many as he could out in the runs and let them exercise for a little while. Feeding time was always a bit of a dance while he made sure each dog got their share and that those who needed medications truly took them. Once everyone was fed, he left them in the runs for more time to stretch their legs and headed out. He knew each building on the property and approached each outbuilding carefully, hoping he didn't scare up any unwanted visitors. The old corn crib was silent, as was the now-empty silo. He checked the floors and around them for any signs of disturbance before moving on. He found nothing and approached the equipment shed.

The door was closed but not locked. Mitchell tried to remember how he had left it the last time he'd been out here. It had been a while. In his father's time, the shed had been where he'd kept the tractors and did the maintenance on them. Now there were only the lawn mowers and garden equipment. Mitchell kept a small utility tractor for larger jobs on the property, but he'd sold most of the equipment when he decided to lease out the land rather than farm it himself. He had used that money to start the shelter. Mostly the building was empty.

Mitchell approached slowly, cautiously. He pulled open the door and stood back in case something happened. No guys in black clothes jumped out, and no hail of bullets whizzed by his ears. He peered around the opening and inside. Nothing seemed out of the ordinary. The lawn mowers and tractor were in their places.

Mitchell entered and wandered through the area. There was nothing that shouldn't be there. The tools were in their places, all on the hooks against the wall the way his father always had them. He passed the tractor and checked behind it. Nothing but floor and dust.

A ladder had fallen onto the floor, and Mitchell picked it up and put it back in its place before leaving the shed and latching the door. That little exercise hadn't yielded much at all. If someone was watching from somewhere on the property, he wasn't sure where it was from.

Mitchell returned to the shelter and got all the dogs inside and into their enclosures. It had been a quiet couple of days for dog adoptions, and he wondered how he was going to get the word out to more people than just the clients of the clinic and his neighbors. Once he was done, Mitchell closed the doors and returned to the house, where he found Beau on the sofa feeding Jessica a bottle.

"You look confused."

"Just trying to figure out how to get the word out about the shelter. I've adopted out a lot of dogs over the years, but I'm at close to capacity now, and I need to find homes for some of the dogs who have been with me for a while."

"Do you have a website?" Beau asked as a knock sounded on the door. Their conversation stalled as Mitchell paid for the food, but resumed as they ate at the coffee table.

"Yes, and pictures and details of all the dogs are on it. I get quite a few pet parents through the site. But I need to do better."

"Social media," Beau suggested. "Create a Facebook page or a group so you can cast a wider net." He smiled and shifted Jessica to his shoulder to burp her. "I also know there's a harvest festival in town. Have you thought about getting a booth and bringing some of the dogs for adoption? They get a lot of people who come through, and I bet a lot of people will adopt. And if you like, I can look at your website to see if we can punch it up." Jessica gave one of her classic "wake the dead" belches, and then he brought her back to his lap and gave her the rest of the bottle.

"That would be great. I have Facebook for myself and stuff, but I suppose I should be doing it for the shelter as well. It would be a lot more productive than me posting about my day and telling people what I had for dinner." He hated to admit that he did that some days because he couldn't think of anything else to post, and it seemed in really bad taste to talk about the types of procedures he had done that day. "My life is so boring most of the time that me posting about my day would put people to sleep."

"Then post pictures of the dogs. People love dog and cat pictures, and it would get you some more exposure." Beau pulled Jessica's bottle away, and she stayed asleep in his arms. Mitchell shifted over and sat next to him with Beau leaning against his shoulder. "You could post details about each dog and what they're like and include a way to contact the shelter. They could message you through Facebook."

"That would be awesome." Though he knew he would have to do more work vetting potential owners. As it was, a lot of the people who adopted his dogs were clients or friends of friends. He wanted to make sure each of his dogs was going to a good home and would be well cared for. "I could also talk to them about the dogs."

"Yeah. I can help you get everything set up, and we can use the website pictures as a start. Maybe take some short videos of the dogs outdoors that you can post and maybe add to the website." Beau slowly shifted Jessica to her carrier. "I really love the things you're doing. I never knew how badly people can treat animals, and I want to try to help. All those dogs out there are so lucky. You care for all of them and spend a lot of your extra time and money to keep them fed and healthy and find them good homes. It's really wonderful and completely selfless." Beau took his hand. "I don't think I can remember the last time I met a truly selfless person."

Mitchell chuckled. "I'm not by a long shot." He glanced at Jessica. "See, right now I'm thinking that I'd like Jessica's daddy to put her to bed, and then maybe he could join me back here on the sofa and the two of us could have some quiet time, maybe a little adult time together." He swallowed hard.

Beau gasped and fanned his face with his hand. "And this is why you offered to let us stay here? So you could get me alone and at your mercy?" He gasped again. "I'm not that kind of guy." His eyes widened dramatically, and then he broke into a fit of laughter. "Let me get her ready for bed." He left the room with a smile.

Mitchell grabbed some fresh clothes from his room, went into the bathroom, and turned on the shower. He stripped down and stepped under the water, intending to wash quickly, but the hot water and his mind derailed that idea. The last few times he had showered, images of Beau had come to him, and this time was no exception. As soon as the water soothed his ragged mind, it switched gears, and Mitchell wondered what it would be like if Beau stepped in behind him. He stifled a moan as his imagination conjured up Beau's arms sliding around his waist, his hot, slick chest pressing to Mitchell's back. He grew hard in seconds and closed his eyes, willing his fantasy to continue.

"Yeah," he whispered to himself as he closed his hand around his length, sliding slowly back and forth, his fantasy getting really good as Beau turned him around, kneeling right in front of him. Mitchell clamped his eyes closed and went with the images in his head. It felt so good and soothed his otherwise jagged nerves. Tightening his grip, he pumped as the imaginary Beau took him between his perfect lips and….

A thump outside the door made him jump slightly, yanking him back to the present. Mitchell sighed and quickly finished his shower, wondering if Beau might need help. He rinsed off, his cock going down when it realized the action was over. After drying off and dressing, he found that Beau was still with Jessica. He went to the living room and turned on the television, keeping the volume low. He really had little idea how long it took to put a baby to bed, but he was surprised when Beau hadn't returned in an hour. Quietly, he approached the guest room, not wanting to disturb them.

Beau's deep voice softly wrapped around him as he sang to his daughter. Mitchell tried to think of anything so touching and couldn't. He peered into the room to where Beau sat on the edge of the bed with Jessica in his arms, rocking slowly as he sang to her. It was a beautiful image, and Mitchell couldn't look away. Mitchell had had so much hurt in his life that at times he had thought his heart completely beyond repair. Yet Beau singing to his daughter touched him in a way he hadn't expected.

Mitchell had known Beau was a kind, gentle man—he'd seen it in the way he treated Randi and Jessica—but this went to a new level. This was loving in a deep way. Mitchell had come to understand, after the way Luke had treated him, that the big things and grand gestures could all be faked. It was the little things, the small touches and quiet gestures, that were for real. They came from deep inside and were a true reflection of the heart.

Randi lay on the bed next to Beau, resting her head on his leg. She raised it, looking at him, and then settled once more. Mitchell backed away and returned downstairs to the living room, where he stared at the television until Beau joined him. "She's sound asleep, and Randi is sleeping at the foot of the bed. I had to move the portacrib a little because I swear Randi would jump in with her if she could." Beau sat next to him, and Mitchell instantly tensed. He knew it was a leftover reaction from Luke, and he made himself relax. Beau wasn't him and didn't play his kind of games. "What are you watching?"

Mitchell handed Beau the remote. "You can pick something. I have Netflix if you want to try to find a movie or something." He sat back and tried to think what he wanted to do. He had already kissed Beau, and his pulse raced at having him this close, but he still found himself second-guessing. He didn't want to push, but Beau had welcomed his advances so far and had even initiated once. That had been cool. God, Mitchell wished he could just shut off the hamster wheel of doubt that sometimes ran in his head. He turned to glance at Beau and found him looking back.

Beau leaned closer, and Mitchell swallowed as Beau came nearer, then stopped and pulled away. "Are you okay?" he breathed. "I'm sorry if I read things wrong. Are things going too fast?"

Mitchell chuckled. "I was going to ask you the same thing. I know it hasn't been that long, and I thought maybe I was moving too fast."

Beau chuckled again, this time smiling brightly. "I guess we were thinking the same thing." He scooted closer and leaned against him. "I know you aren't Gerome and that all guys don't act the way he does. It's stupid of me to paint everyone with the same brush."

Mitchell nodded and sighed. "Doesn't stop the worry and the wondering, though." He put an arm around Beau. "I keep thinking that there's something wrong with me and I don't trust my own judgment. Maybe I have bad taste or something."

"Is that what you think?" Beau asked, turning toward him. "Am I a result of your bad taste?"

Mitchell knew Beau was kidding… but not completely. The doubts could run wild, regardless of whether they had any factual basis. “No. You are definitely not that.” Beau slid nearer.

Their lips touched softly at first, and then Beau slid his hands around the back of his head, deepening the kiss. Mitchell slid closer, eliminating the gap between them, Beau’s heat surrounding him, his scent intensifying as the room grew smaller and the air heavy with desire. Beau’s lips were firm and just wet enough to be perfect. He tasted rich with a hint of sweetness that drew Mitchell like ambrosia. He didn’t want to stop. He pressed closer, pushing both of them down toward the cushions.

Mitchell stopped and backed away before they ended up on the floor. He inhaled deeply, trying to calm his racing heart. This had always been his problem. Once he got to this stage with a guy, he’d always figured it was full steam ahead, and that was when everything went to hell. He and Luke had moved really quickly at the beginning, and before he’d even realized it, Mitchell had given away his heart, moved in, and let Luke become the center of his life. But this wasn’t Luke, and Beau was a completely different kind of man. He swallowed as a sour taste filled his throat. “I….”

Beau stroked his cheek. “What is it? Do you think I’m like him?”

“No. I don’t. But if I close my eyes, sometimes I imagine him with me, looking over my shoulder or something.” It was almost like his ghost was along for the ride.

"I know what you mean. I felt like Gerome was always with me until I stood up to him and told him to leave me alone. Up until that point, it always felt like Gerome was the one controlling my life."

Shit.... Mitchell's head spun as the reality of what Beau had just said rang true. Mitchell had gotten away from Luke, but even after all these years, he hadn't stood up to him. Mitchell had tried to move on with his life, but there hadn't been any closure. Here he was, worried about how things would be for Beau, when he was the one with the unresolved issues. Maybe there truly was something wrong with him. It had been years since he'd gotten away from Luke and built his own life. It wasn't like Luke was a constant presence in his mind. He rarely thought about him. But that was before he'd met Beau. Now Luke had become a constant presence in his head again, and he hated it. The guy should be gone! Mitchell clenched a fist against the cushion.

"You're lucky," Mitchell said softly. "But I also know you aren't Luke and aren't going to treat me the way he did." He swallowed around a lump that threatened to cut off his ability to speak. "I thought I had come to terms with all this."

"Do you think I have? Who knows? I suspect there are going to be times when Gerome is going to reappear, especially when I finally think he's gone for good."

"Exactly. The assholes in our lives will make regular appearances, especially when we're least prepared for it. I thought mine was gone, so naturally he rears his ugly head inside my mind once more." Mitchell turned to Beau. "I don't want him to color things with you." He took Beau's hand and entwined their fingers. "I want to try and see where things go. To give us a chance."

Beau nodded. "I want that too." Mitchell leaned forward and kissed him. Who knew what was going to happen next, but at least Mitchell had taken one step farther than he ever had PL—post Luke.

Chapter 8

BEAU LOVED kissing. It was one of his favorite things, and Mitchell's sent tingles up and down his spine. While Mitchell held him, Beau explored slowly, tentatively, their kisses heating once more.

When they broke apart, breathing deeply, Beau looked intensely into Mitchell's eyes. He had heard that the eyes were the window to the soul, and Mitchell's were no different. Where Mitchell was open, Gerome had been closed, and where Mitchell's were kind and soft, Gerome's had been like stone, cold and hard. Looking back, Beau should have realized that there had been something wrong, but he hadn't put it all together, and that was probably his fault. He had wanted to see what was good—and he had, until it was no longer possible. Beau was determined that he wasn't going to make the same mistake again, and that meant that he needed to keep his head in the game and not let himself get carried away, but it was hard with Mitchell. He seemed to get under all Beau's defenses.

"What are you watching?"

"You," Beau answered. "I think I'm trying to find the answers to questions that I don't know how to ask." That probably didn't make a lot of sense, but it was the best explanation he could come up with. Beau sat back, putting some distance between them. It was hard to think with Mitchell so close. "I should probably go to bed. Jessica will be up a couple times during the night, and…." He kissed Mitchell and made an escape, because if he didn't leave right this moment, he was likely to do something he wasn't ready for.

This entire situation was throwing him for a loop, but he wasn't sure how to tell Mitchell. He had told the truth, that he had felt better and a lot more in control since he'd confronted Gerome, but he'd displayed a lot more confidence than he felt. Beau didn't think that Mitchell was anything like Gerome, but sometimes it felt like he was walking on quicksand, and he wasn't quite sure how to handle all the changes in his life.

What he really needed was a chance to think and figure stuff out. Maybe staying here for the night was a bad idea, but Beau was afraid that Gerome was out there watching him, and he needed to make sure Jessica was safe. That was his top priority.

He closed the guest room door and sat on the side of the bed without turning on the lights. He didn't want to make a sound and wake the baby, and this was the one place he knew he could be alone with his thoughts.

Randi came over, pranced onto his lap, and placed her paws on his chest. Beau took a deep breath to calm his nerves, wondering if he was being a complete and total fool. When they'd been kissing, he'd felt Mitchell's excitement. It was hard to miss. He was pretty sure if he crossed the hall and joined Mitchell in his bedroom, he would be welcome.

"I don't know what I should do," he whispered to Randi. All his thoughts seemed to have melded together in a jumbled mess that refused to slow down.

A soft knock startled him, and Randi jumped down to the floor. Beau opened the door in case she started barking and woke Jessica.

Mitchell stood framed in the dim light from the hallway. "I'm sorry if I made you uncomfortable or went too fast or something."

Beau met him in the hall, closing the door most of the way behind him. "You didn't," he whispered. "Not really. Sometimes I just can't seem to figure out how to keep my thoughts and worries from taking over. I know it sounds dumb, but…."

Mitchell set his hand on his shoulder. "That happens to me too." He smiled. "It sounds like you and I are both bumbling around in the dark trying to figure stuff out and not wanting to step on the other's toes." That was as good a description as any as far as Beau could figure out. Mitchell took his hand and guided him a few steps away. Randi wandered off toward the kitchen, and Beau lifted his gaze, Mitchell's drawing his full attention. "What is it you really want? Don't worry about me or what you think I might want. Just tell me what it is you want most."

Beau hesitated for a second and then pulled Mitchell to him, pushed him against the wall, and proceeded to kiss the hell out of him. Mitchell had said to tell him what he wanted, and Beau figured he couldn't have painted a clearer picture if he tried.

Mitchell closed his arms around him, returning the kiss with enough heat to melt Beau's shoes. Damn, he was hot. Beau let Mitchell guide him across the hall and into the master bedroom. "Wait…," Beau whispered, pulling away as soon as the door closed behind them.

"What is it?" Mitchell asked, stilling. In the dim light he looked like a teenager, all nerves and excitement. "What's wrong?"

"Nothing." Beau went through a mental checklist. Jessica was asleep just across the hall, and he had the baby monitor. The house was quiet, and he wanted this. "Everything is fine." He sat on the edge of the bed. "It's just that the last few months, whenever I think things are okay, that's when everything goes to hell, and I wanted to make sure that there was nothing looming at the moment." He smiled. "I can't think of anything."

Mitchell leaned over the bed, his hands on each of Beau's knees, drawing closer. Their lips met, and Mitchell pressed him back onto the mattress. Beau sprawled and drew Mitchell down with him, holding him tightly as Mitchell's weight held him against the bedding. "You know, we said that we should take things slowly, and yet this…."

"I've gone slow," Mitchell said. "I wanted to do this—" He licked the base of Beau's neck, sending heat racing through him like a freight train. "—since our first kiss. You taste like ambrosia, and I've wondered if the rest of you was the same." He popped the first buttons on Beau's shirt and parted the fabric, his lips doing incredible things to the exposed skin. Beau held on as Mitchell set him on fire. He was damned excited. His pants were suddenly way too tight, and all he could think about was the fact that he was warm, cared for, and that Mitchell hadn't even removed his clothes and he was already so damned close to the edge that if he didn't get himself under control he was going to go off in his pants—and that hadn't happened since he was a teenager.

"Mitchell," Beau breathed. "God…." He uncrossed his eyes and now, seeing straight, looked into Mitchell's. Damn, he was gorgeous. Beau could get lost in those deep, beautiful, caring eyes. "You're going to make me lose it if you aren't careful."

"You?" Mitchell smiled, drawing his lips closer once again. "I can't get enough of you." Beau scoffed lightly. "Really. Remember that first day when I came over to be nice because you had complained about the dogs, and…."

Beau felt his cheeks heat. "And you're bringing that up now because…?" He felt bad enough about that.

"You opened the door with Jessica crying on your shoulder, and all I could think was how great you looked and that I was jealous of a little baby because she got to touch you. I know it sounds dumb, but my fingers actually tingled."

"I was a complete mess. Jessica had been up for hours, and I hadn't slept in days. There must have been roller bags under my eyes…."

"And you were gorgeous." Mitchell kissed away his retort, and for a second Beau wondered if maybe there was something wrong with Mitchell's judgment if he thought that was sexy. But then after two seconds of Mitchell pressing to him once again, working open his shirt and slipping a hot hand along his chest, Beau forgot about everything other than that heated touch.

His lips tingled, and he inhaled sharply when Mitchell pulled them away. "Don't stop." He felt alive for the first time in months. It was like Mitchell was clearing away the cobwebs and dust left over from the crash and burn of his previous relationship, and damn, he needed that so badly.

"I have no intention… unless you tell me to." Mitchell locked their gazes, and Beau whimpered softly, needing more. His hips shifted because damn, he was getting desperate as waves of excitement rolled through him, crashing against his mind again and again.

"Not going to happen." Beau slipped his arms around Mitchell's neck and tugged him down. As far as he was concerned, the talking portion of the evening was over, and it was time for the moaning and gasping to begin—which Beau did until his throat was dry.

Mitchell seemed to have a sixth sense about what Beau liked and just how far to take it before pulling back. They hadn't even undressed and Beau was panting, his hands shaking as he tugged at the hem of Mitchell's shirt. Beau needed this off. When it seemed to fight him, he rolled them on the bed and straddled Mitchell's body, got the shirt over his head, and raked his gaze down Mitchell's body.

"Damn," he muttered, taking in his pale skin, the dash of light hair in the center of his chest, trim, lean muscles, and pert nipples that just begged to teased. "You weren't the only one with an active imagination, although mine seems to have fallen a little short of reality." He cradled Mitchell's cheeks in his hands, leaned closer, and kissed him while Mitchell wrapped strong, bare arms around him.

"I want you naked," Mitchell breathed during a brief kissing break and proceeded to deftly divest Beau of his pants. They got caught on his shoes, but Beau kicked the whole mess off before yanking Mitchell's belt away and getting rid of the pesky pair of jeans. After all the machinations and refusal to be apart, they were finally bare to each other, and Mitchell held him tightly, sliding his hands up and down Beau's back until they cupped his buttcheeks, sliding up and over them.

"You have magic hands," Beau whispered.

"That's not all that's magic," Mitchell retorted.

Beau snickered. "God, that was really bad," he said with a smile, Mitchell's eyes dancing with delight. "You're really making a dick joke at a time like this?" He rolled his eyes.

"I wasn't joking," Mitchell deadpanned.

"I see." This was fun. He had never been with someone playful in bed. Gerome was always serious and ready to get down to business. "Well, are you going to enlighten me with the particular brand of magic that is Mitchell?" He grinned quickly and then closed the distance between them.

Mitchell shifted them on the bed, once again pressing Beau into the mattress. Beau loved Mitchell's weight on top of him and the way their heat melded together. He really did have magic hands, and when those fingers closed around his cock, stroking slowly, it was maddening, like Beau's head was going to explode if he just got a little more friction. Beau breathed deeply, perspiration breaking out as he wondered how he was going to keep himself from flying apart. Then the deliciousness stopped, and Beau wondered what was going on. "Why did you stop?"

A chuckle reached his ears as Mitchell slid down him. Then Beau was engulfed in hot, wet heat that sent his mind flying toward the stratosphere. Thinking about anything flew out the window. Mitchell was indeed magic… and gifted, judging by the fact that he took all of Beau so easily. Beau moaned loudly, trying not to make noise and failing completely. "Mitchell… I…. Jesus…." Stars formed behind his eyes, and he gripped the bedding in his fists, trying to stop himself from flying to pieces.

"Did I lie?" Mitchell asked, Beau's cock bouncing against his belly.

"No…," he whimpered, breathlessly. "But…."

Mitchell kissed him. "Just lie back and relax. You don't need to worry about anything." Mitchell smoothed his hands down Beau's chest, hot breath following in their wake, and then sucked him down once more.

Beau's leg shook with ecstasy. He hoped this never ended, but it seemed his traitorous body had its own ideas. Before he could stop himself, his entire body tingled. Beau managed to whimper a warning before his release slammed into him.

A rag doll had nothing on Beau when he lay back on Mitchell's bed, his eyes closed, heart still beating fast but slowly returning to its normal speed. "I think I died and went to heaven. If you give me a minute, I'll…."

Mitchell chuckled close to his ear, his weight settling next to him. "Um… I already…. You were hot, and things got a little out of hand for me." He rested his head on Beau's shoulder, both of them still breathing heavily. "You're a real firecracker."

"I've never been told that before." Beau kind of liked it. The idea that Mitchell found him attractive was hot. Beau had never thought of himself as someone's ideal guy. "But the hotness in the room lies with you." He could watch Mitchell all day. He held him closer.

"You're tensing."

"I don't mean to. But Jessica is going to be waking up in a few hours." Beau closed his eyes as Mitchell got up, quietly leaving the room. When he returned again, a warm cloth skimmed lightly over Beau's belly, and they got under the covers and Mitchell turned out the light. "I should check on her." Beau got out from under the soft covers and trudged across the hall. Jessica was sound asleep in her portacrib, with Randi at the foot of the bed, watching over her. Beau stroked Randi gently before leaving the room once again. "She's sleeping like an angel."

Mitchell held up the covers, and Beau dropped off to sleep almost as soon as his head hit the pillow. He hadn't fallen asleep like that in a long time. Maybe he did feel safe here.

BEAU WOKE with a start and checked the clock near the bed. It was three in the morning, and he was alone. Beau jumped out of bed and hurried to the guest room, where he found Mitchell with Jessica in his arms. He was sitting on the side of the bed, holding the last of a bottle, with Jessica sound asleep. The sight made him pause. There had been very few times in his life when a sight so beautiful stopped him in his tracks. Mitchell was bare-chested, dressed in boxers, and Jessica was so adorable in his arms. "I didn't want to wake you. I figured you could use the rest. I changed her, and she's ready to go back to bed." Mitchell gently placed her in the crib and then turned back to him. "Go on back to bed. I'll be right in."

"Where are you going?" Beau asked.

"I'm just going to take care of these few things and then I'll join you in bed." Mitchell hurried away with the diaper and empty bottle.

Beau returned to the bedroom and got under the covers. Mitchell came in and slid right up behind him, gliding a hand over his belly. Mitchell tugged him closer. "Just go to sleep. Everything is fine. Jessica will hopefully sleep for a few more hours." He caressed Beau's arm, and the tension that had seemed to be an inescapable companion ever since Jessica came to him slipped away, at least for a little while.

BEAU ACTUALLY slept hard. He woke with light coming through the windows as Jessica cried out from the other room. Mitchell was still asleep when he slipped out of the bed. Beau got Jessica out of the crib and took her out to the other room along with the diaper bag. He changed her on the sofa and then got a bottle while she cried, tears running down her cheeks, until he got the formula the right temperature. The crying came to abrupt halt with the bottle. She sucked like her life depended on it.

"Poor little thing," Beau whispered to her. "You were completely starving." She always seemed to eat like she hadn't seen food for days. He knew that was a good thing. Jessica's healthy appetite was better than the alternative, where she was finicky and he had to try to coax her to eat.

After taking Jessica into the living room, he sat on the sofa and got comfortable. There was something soothing about feeding her, almost like yoga. She was happy, and his mind got a chance to wander a little in the quiet. It took a little trip back to the bedroom where Mitchell lay sleeping. Beau swallowed hard, pulling himself out of the flight of fancy as he sat Jessica upright and gently burped her before giving her the bottle once again.

"I was wondering where you'd gotten off to," Mitchell said as he shuffled into the room in a pair of shorts. "I woke up to an empty bed. I figured this little princess must have been hungry."

"She was. I'm surprised she didn't wake you." He watched Jessica's eyes drift closed now that her belly was getting full. "I know that you have to feed the dogs and then get to the clinic. I'll get our stuff packed and head on home." He yawned widely and was unable to cover it. "I feel a lot better this morning. Maybe what I really needed was a good night's sleep to stop feeling so paranoid all the time."

"You don't need to rush off."

Beau nodded. "Thanks, but I have work I need to do, and I know you do as well." He needed a chance to think about last night and the way Mitchell made him feel. Damn, it would be so easy to fall for this man—he was gentle and caring—but the truth was that Beau didn't trust his own judgment. "I also have some calls to make to my lawyer. He's working to put the property in Philadelphia up for sale for me." He suspected that movement on that front was why Gerome had been trying to get even with him. "It still makes me angry, what happened to Randi."

"It looks like she's going to be fine." Mitchell sat down next to him. "You need to promise me that you'll call if you see or even suspect that anyone is hanging around. The next time, we'll call the police and get them out to look around. That might scare off whoever is behind this if they know the police are involved." He sighed. "I want you to be safe."

"I will be. And you need to do the same." Beau didn't want anything to happen to Mitchell either. If someone hurt his dog and was watching him, then they would know about Mitchell and might try to hurt him too. The idea sent a cold shiver up Beau's back.

"I'm going to get dressed, and then I'll take you and Sleeping Beauty home."

MITCHELL HELPED Beau carry his things into the house and had a look around before getting ready to leave for the clinic. "Call me if anything happens."

Beau smiled. "I will, I promise." Mitchell kissed him, and this was no simple goodbye kiss, but one that made him tingle and contained a promise of more to come. Beau liked that. He stood holding Jessica and watched out the front window until Mitchell got into his car and drove off. With a sigh, he buckled

Jessica into her swing. He figured he could try to get some work done while she was occupied.

One thing that Beau had had to do was change his way of working. Instead of getting long bouts of time where he could concentrate, he had had to re-train his mind to work in quick, short bursts. He usually got a few hours once Jessica was in bed, but the rest of his work was completed in half-hour increments throughout the day. It should probably drive him crazy, but it was a necessity.

"You doing okay, sweetheart?" Beau asked when he came up for air after making strides on his project. Jessica was quiet, her eyes closed. Randi lay near her feet. She was so cute when she slept. Beau returned to work, figuring that as long as she was content, he'd take advantage of it.

Thoughts of Mitchell invaded as he turned back to his computer. His fingers hovered over the keyboard as he remembered the way Mitchell's hands glided over his skin. Heat followed wherever Mitchell touched, and Beau closed his eyes, his mind floating on the glorious memory, savoring it and the way Mitchell had made him feel completely alive and whole again. Gerome had ripped away a part of him, and Beau felt like that missing piece was returning.

Beau growled at himself. He hated when Gerome intruded on everything in his life. What he and Mitchell had experienced the night before was beautiful. It sent his heart soaring… and Beau hated that he even thought of Gerome at all. He pushed him aside in his mind while part of him wished he could just push Gerome off a cliff somewhere and get him the hell out of his life and head forever. That wasn't going to happen, but Beau was determined to keep him out of his mind as much as possible.

He returned to work but had to stop again when Jessica began to fuss. Beau saved everything and went to pick her up. She stopped immediately, and he rocked her as he walked the room. He checked her diaper before getting a bottle. She ate like she was starved.

Beau was just burping her when a firm knock made him jump. He felt uneasy as he peered out the window and then opened the door to an older man and woman. "Can I help you?"

A man with salt-and-pepper hair, piercing eyes, and a commanding demeanor stepped forward. "My wife and I are here to see our granddaughter."

Chapter 9

"SOMEONE IS extra happy this morning," Bonnie said between patients as she cleaned the examination area and Mitchell got ready for his next appointment.

"Why wouldn't I be? What kind of appointment is better than a litter of beagle puppies in for their first checkup?" There were parts of his job that he just adored, and that was one of them. The five pups were doing well and as cute as buttons. You couldn't help but smile.

"It's more than that," she teased, her smile radiant. "If I wanted to speculate, I'd say you got lucky." She giggled like a teenager, and Mitchell rolled his eyes. "You did. You're blushing." She paused in her task. "Dang. That Beau is one cool drink of water. I know I wouldn't kick him out of bed for eating crackers."

"Quit gossiping," Mitchell chastised.

"It's not gossip if it's true, and besides, you're right here. I could go out and talk to Val to see what she thinks." Dang, Bonnie was in rare form today, and Mitchell wasn't sure how he felt about it. He and Beau had had an amazing night and his cheeks were still heated, but he didn't think he wanted everyone knowing. It left him feeling exposed, and he hated it. Most of all he hated Luke for it.

"Just finish up, please." He wasn't angry with her, but some of his joy had slipped away. Fuck it all, he should be able to be happy about how things were with Beau, and yet it made him nervous. And it shouldn't.

Bonnie watched him as though she were trying to figure something out.

"Dr. Brannigan?" Val said as she stuck her head in. Mitchell was grateful for the break and the fact that Bonnie's grilling was at an end. "There's a call for you. It's your young man, and he seems really upset."

Mitchell swallowed and nodded. "I'll be right there."

Val closed the door.

"I got this," Bonnie told him, and Mitchell left the exam room and picked up the phone in front.

"Beau?"

"They're here," he said breathily. "They showed up a little while ago."

"Who?" Mitchell was ready to leave and race to his car for the trip back. "What's happened?"

The line was silent except for Beau's heavy breathing. "Jessica's grandparents. They knocked on my door an hour ago."

"Amy's parents?" Mitchell asked. It didn't make sense to him. Beau would most likely have known them if Amy was that good a friend.

"No. The father's parents, Helen and Franklin van der Spoel. Their son signed away his rights, but they aren't happy about it and they wanted to see their granddaughter. They keep looking at my house and whispering to each other." He seemed beside himself.

"Do they have Jessica?" he asked, concerned that they could try to take her away or something, especially if they were left alone with her.

"No. I left the room with her because she was getting fussy, and it's the first chance I've had to call you." He sounded half panicked.

"Did you ask for ID? Do you know these people at all? Have you met them before?" Mitchell asked.

"No. They seem nice enough, and she sounds just like she did on the phone, but they creep me out too. They seem to think they have rights and that I should just roll over to do what they want." Beau's nerves practically jangled through the line.

Mitchell wished he could get over there right away. "Ask them to leave, and if they don't, dial 911. You can sort it out later. But these are strangers, and they want to see your daughter." He grew agitated and looked at Val.

"I can go over," she volunteered.

Mitchell nodded. "Go," he told her, then returned to the phone. "Val is on her way. I have appointments, but you'll have someone else in the house besides you." Val had already gathered her purse and left the office. "She's leaving the office right now."

"Good. I don't want to hang up." Jessica began crying in the background, and rustling came through the line. "I need to change Jessica and get her a bottle, and…."

"It's okay. Like I said, Val is already driving over and should be there in a few minutes." He turned to the door as his next appointment arrived with her yowling cat. Mitchell greeted her and said he would be with her in a few minutes. He turned away and stayed with Beau until the doorbell sounded over the phone. "That's Val."

"Thank goodness. I got her changed and need to get her bottle. I'll call you when they leave." Beau seemed so nervous, but he hung up, and Mitchell put the phone in its cradle and returned to work, hoping everything was okay. He really wished he could hurry out of the clinic, but he had appointments.

"Please come on back," he told Mrs. Weaver, and she brought the crying Whiskers back with her. He examined Whiskers and gave him his shot. Once he was done, he saw them to the door and called Beau. "Are you okay?"

"Yes." He sounded much calmer. "They left almost as soon as Val arrived. I think she intimidated them."

"Did they say what they wanted?" Mitchell asked.

Beau sighed. "They told me that they just wanted to see their granddaughter. I'm not sure how they found me." He paused, and Mitchell checked the lobby, which was empty, and was grateful for the lull in his day. "I'm not convinced they were being truthful, though. They cooed over Jessica, and I really think they were who they said they were. But they want something. I know it. They kept talking quietly between them and watching me all the time like I had two heads. Helen asked to hold Jessica, but I didn't allow it until Val arrived, and then we both sat in the room."

"Sounds really tense," Mitchell said.

"It was strange. I mean, who shows up at someone's house unannounced to visit and then practically barges in like they have some sort of right to be there? I kept hinting that I had work to do, but they ignored me. Val finally told them that I had an appointment and that they had to leave."

"All right. I'll stop by after I finish work. Jeremy is at my place now, seeing to the dogs for me." He didn't want Beau to be alone. Mitchell could only image how vulnerable he must be feeling. But Mitchell had people coming out on adoption appointments—things had suddenly gotten very busy for him.

"Thank you. I'm trying to figure out what they could want."

"I'll be there as soon as I can."

"YOU SHOULD have done more!" Alan March said as he stomped around the examination room. "You just let him die." Mitchell thought the middle-aged man was going to hit him any second.

"Please calm down. Ricky was very old, and the cancer had just spread too far. There was nothing I could have done." Mitchell hated when an animal was beyond hope. Alan had waited too long and now the man had arrived in a panic with a golden retriever literally breathing his last. "You gave him a good life."

"I did, and now it's over, no thanks to you," Alan snapped.

"That's enough," Val said as she came in. "Alan March, you behave and don't yell at the doctor. He isn't a miracle worker, and you don't get to be an ass here." She put her hands on her hips, glaring him down. "Margaret would be so ashamed of you."

"Don't you dare bring her up," Alan retorted as he scooped Ricky up off the table. "I still say he could have helped Ricky. You doctors are all the same." He charged out of the examination room, cradling the body of his dog as though it were precious. "This isn't over."

The front door of the clinic slammed so hard Mitchell jumped and the building shook around him. Val patted him on the shoulder and returned to the reception area. Mitchell took a deep breath and did his best to get his mind back on track. He'd dealt with this kind of loss before, and he knew the anger that came along with it.

"I'm sorry, Doctor. Alan has always had a short fuse and a raw temper. Ever since his wife died, it's gotten worse, and he lashes out at everyone," Val said once he joined her in the now-empty reception area. "He was a good man once, but I think now all that's left is loneliness and hatred for the entire world and everyone in it."

"Do you think he'll… do anything about it?" Mitchell asked.

Val shrugged. "Most likely he'll go home, bury his dog, and probably get himself drunk to try to forget. But I'd watch things the next couple of days to be sure. He's unpredictable." She gave him a half smile, and Mitchell wondered how he got himself into these things. He'd only been trying to help someone who walked into his clinic. Sometimes there was nothing he could do.

"Thanks," he said, not wanting Val to worry, and got busy when his next appointment arrived.

After that, everything took longer than he expected. Mitchell had an additional walk-in emergency. By the time he was done and had closed up the clinic, he was exhausted and starving. He headed home to check on the dogs. It had started raining a few hours before, so all the dogs were inside. The happy, excited cacophony of barks and yips when he came into the barn was nearly deafening. They were all excited, and once his adoption appointment arrived, the din grew even louder.

"My…," the young lady, Lynn, said while they talked.

"The pack is a little cooped up, so they have extra energy right now." He smiled and showed her each of the dogs until she came to an abrupt stop.

"Who is this?" she asked.

Mitchell grinned. "That's Sweetiepie. She was injured, and it wasn't treated until too late." He took her out of the enclosure, and Sweetiepie came right up to Lynn and nuzzled her hand for pets. "She's the sweetest dog and so gentle." His heart beat a little faster. "Sweetiepie gets around really well now, and she's so good with people. She's been with me for about six months. I've been hoping to find her a home, but it hasn't happened yet."

Lynn drew Sweetiepie closer. "Until today. I think she was waiting for me." Mitchell's entire body tingled, and danged if he didn't rub his eyes. "She's the one for me." Lynn stood. "I assume there's some paperwork I need to fill out. How much does she cost?"

Mitchell swallowed. "We charge just enough to cover our overall costs for feed, shelter, shots, and general care. That's all. My job is to find them good homes. If you'd like to make a donation to help feed and care for the dogs, that would be appreciated as well." He was always low-key when it came to that part of the process, but it didn't faze Lynn, and she wrote him a nice-sized check and handed it over without batting an eye.

"Do you need help?" Lynn asked as she straightened up. "My husband and I love dogs. Our last one passed away three months ago, and our house has been very empty. Sweetiepie will be greatly loved, I can assure you of that. But I have to ask how you afford to do all this? The fees can't be enough."

"I supplement the shelter through the clinic. I just can't let these animals be put to sleep or suffer. It's important that they find homes and be loved."

Lynn nodded. "You're doing good work." She handed him a business card. "Call me. I work for the Harrison Foundation in Harrisburg, and we give a number of grants to promote community service. You should apply for one."

"Mitchell?"

He turned to see Beau standing in the barn doorway holding Jessica in one arm and an umbrella in his hand.

Mitchell couldn't help smiling. "What are you doing out here in this weather?" He hurried over, ushered Beau inside, and closed the umbrella. "You're going to get wet."

"I tried calling, but you didn't answer, and I got worried. So I came over…." He noticed Lynn and Sweetiepie at that moment. "I'm sorry. I should have known you were busy." He seemed pale and nervous.

"It's okay. This is Lynn and her newly adopted dog. This is my boyfriend, Beau, and his daughter Jessica." He had to stop himself from touching her little head. He was covered in dog and didn't want to get Jessica dirty.

"I should be going. But definitely apply. This is certainly a worthy endeavor," Lynn said. Mitchell got a leash and snapped it onto Sweetiepie's collar.

Lynn led her out of the barn and to her car. Sweetiepie climbed in, and Lynn waved before turning the car around and heading out of the drive.

"You're going to miss her," Beau said gently.

Mitchell nodded. "I've had her longer than any other dog." He swallowed hard. "I always told myself that I shouldn't get emotionally attached to any of the dogs in my care. I was supposed to find them homes, and yet…." He closed the door and turned away. "She'll be happy and have a family of her own, a forever home. I know it. That's what she deserves." So why did he feel like a part of himself was being driven away? This was what he did—he found homes for his dogs.

Beau nodded slowly. "You weren't honest with yourself. She was the one you should have brought into your home as your own dog. She already had your heart, but you didn't know it until now. Randi is Jessica's dog, but I think Sweetiepie was yours."

Mitchell sighed. "You talk like we have a doggie soul mate or something." His phone chimed in his pocket. He checked the message, and just as he expected, the other couple he had been waiting for asked to come later because of the weather. Still, it was a good day. "Come on. Let's get the two of you inside, and you can tell me everything that happened." He made sure all the dogs had food and water before turning out the lights and closing the doors.

The rain had picked up, and Mitchell held the umbrella, keeping Beau and Jessica dry in the deluge as they walked to the house. Once inside, he put on some coffee and got Beau settled in the living room, then brought in mugs with dogs on them and set them on the table. "Please, tell me everything." He pulled up the site for the best pizza in town and placed an order while Beau got comfortable.

Beau explained how they arrived. "They had their noses in the air most of the time. Helen was dressed like she was going to a garden party and had a diamond ring the size of Jessica's fist, I swear. Franklin kept pulling his coat around him like he would pick up something from my furniture. They were both edgy, and whenever they thought I wasn't paying attention, they shared these looks like they'd tasted something bad."

"Did they say anything to you?" Mitchell asked.

"Oh, when I was in the room, they asked a lot of questions about Amy and me. They asked if we were married, but I explained that I had been her best friend and she asked me to care for Jessica if anything happened to her. That caused another of those silent conversations."

"And you're sure their son signed away all his rights?" Mitchell said.

Beau nodded. "I found a copy of the paperwork in Amy's things. I have it in the safe-deposit box. I figured if he came around, I'd send him on his way. There's nothing he can do to change that." Beau slowly rocked Jessica. "But I keep wondering what happens if they decide to go after her. I've been sitting alone for hours and wondering if they could take

Jessica away." He bit his lower lip. "They didn't sign anything away, and they are Jessica's blood relatives." He practically shook. "I won't let anyone take her away. Amy wanted me to care for Jessica, and she's my daughter now. I'm her daddy, and I won't give her up. I'll fight those uptight pricks from here to doomsday before I'll let that happen." Mitchell loved the fire in Beau's eyes.

"I don't think they can do that," Mitchell said. He hurried to his computer. "I'm looking at a family law forum online, and there is a grandparents' rights statute in this state. It says they can petition for custody or visitation if they have a relationship with the child, preferably one that's lasted more than twelve months and with the permission of the parent. As far as we know, they have never seen her before today. So they can be as snooty as they want, but they don't have any rights as far as Jessica is concerned." He still wondered what they wanted. "What bothers me is why they would think they could just show up like that?"

Beau shook his head. "I have no idea, but I don't think I want them in my house again. I don't like them." He put Jessica over his shoulder and gently patted her back. "Maybe I'm being paranoid, but I keep thinking somehow that because I'm gay, someone is going to try to take her away."

"I know a couple of good lawyers, and if we need to, we can get you some powerful legal help." He wasn't going to let some strangers hurt Beau or little Jessica. Mitchell shifted closer, and Beau leaned against him. "I'm going to do what I can to keep you safe." They had both already been through too much hell.

"But…."

Mitchell closed the gap between them. "I don't want anything to happen to the two of you. You're a family, and you deserve to be happy and not have people trying to pull you apart."

Mitchell hadn't even thought about it, but he realized he was jealous big-time. He had always wanted a family of his own. His parents were gone, and he had been alone for a long time. Maybe that was part of why he'd opened the shelter. The dogs gave unconditional love, and maybe he'd been looking for that. Beau had that kind of love with Jessica. They both gave it to each other, and it was beautiful. To have someone threaten that made Mitchell's pulse race and his anger rise.

He cared for Beau. It was too early for him to make declarations. Beau most likely wasn't ready for it. Hell, Mitchell wasn't sure if he was ready, but one thing he was certain of: Beau had created this little family of two, and that was pretty special.

"But I worry. Jessica is my daughter. I know I wasn't part of her conception and she isn't a blood relation, but she's part of my heart." Beau sighed raggedly. "Before she came to live with me, I couldn't see myself as a parent. I mean, it wasn't something I thought about. And now that she's here, I can't imagine my life without her. The thought of someone coming into our lives to try to hurt her or take her away scares the crap out of me."

Mitchell could understand that. "You're her daddy. That's part of the job." He had been worried that Beau might not have been ready to care about someone again, but he already did. His heart was open, and it hadn't been Mitchell who had done that but little Jessica. How could anyone possibly keep their heart closed with that little girl around?

Jessica began fussing, and Mitchell grabbed the diaper bag from near the door and pulled out one of the bottles. He warmed it in some hot water in the kitchen and handed it to Beau, who fed her. She stopped after half the bottle, and Beau set it on the coffee table with a yawn.

"Do you want to lie down for a little while?" He offered to hold Jessica, and Beau gently handed her over. Mitchell shifted to the chair as Beau stretched out on the sofa. He slowly got up and got a blanket, which he placed over Beau. Then he sat back down and stretched out himself. Mitchell enjoyed the closeness and warmth of Jessica's little body and how she just accepted him and trusted him. There was no whining or worry, just contentment and going to sleep. This little one was working her way into his heart as well, and Mitchell wondered what he would do if things didn't work out with Beau.

"She's already got you wrapped around her little finger, doesn't she?" Beau asked.

"I think she does, and so does her daddy." He winked, and Beau pulled up the covers, smiling softly. Mitchell closed his eyes and relaxed, letting contentment wash over him. Beau extended his arm, and Mitchell slid his hand into his, staying quiet, just being together for a while. "When I was a kid, I asked my mother how she knew that my dad was the one for her," Mitchell said softly, easily recalling the conversation.

"What was your mom like?" Beau asked.

Mitchell smiled. "My dad said that when she was young, Mom was a wild child. She never did anything she was supposed to do. Apparently she had quite a reputation." He sighed softly. "But Mom always said she just wanted to have a good time, and she wasn't afraid to go out and find it. That was Mom. She never sat still for anyone or anything. Go, go, go, until the day she couldn't anymore." He sighed softly, remembering her. "But when I asked her how she knew Dad was the one, she told me it was because she felt comfortable doing nothing with him. I didn't get it." Mitchell lightly squeezed Beau's hand. The wind rattled the windows, and rain spattered the glass before quieting once again. "She told me that she knew she had met the right person when he just wanted to spent quiet time with her. I guess no one had ever done that before… until my dad."

Beau chuckled softly. "Is that what we're doing here?"

Mitchell shrugged. "I think it just happened." He stood as he heard footsteps on the porch and gently transferred Jessica to her daddy's chest. She curled right up, not waking, as he hurried to the front door before the delivery guy could ring the bell.

Mitchell pulled the door open.

"I have your pizza," the guy said.

Mitchell handed him a cash tip. "Thanks for coming out on a night like this."

He stepped away and then paused as Mitchell was about to close the door. "The door is open on that building, and it's swinging in the wind." He pointed, and Mitchell went to the end of the porch and peered out toward the old equipment shed. Sure enough, the door was open. Cold raced up his spine. Someone had been out there. Mitchell clearly remembered latching the door well, and it wasn't going to just blow open.

"Thank you for letting me know." He smiled, and the delivery man hurried back to his car in an attempt to stay dry. Mitchell took the pizzas inside, grabbed a coat and umbrella, and told Beau that he'd be right back. Then he raced outside and over to the equipment shed. He pulled the door shut and latched it again, hoping to hell nothing jumped out at him in the darkness. The rain increased, pounding around him. Mitchell huddled under the umbrella as the wind threatened to rip it away. He headed across the yard, watching around him. He stopped at the shelter.

The dogs were barking like crazy as he pulled open the door. Mitchell wondered if someone was inside. They were going nuts. Buster tried to make a break for it. Mitchell managed to stop him and closed the door to a roving pack of loose dogs clamoring around him. Shit and hell, someone had opened all the enclosures. "Come on, guys, settle down." He started picking up the little ones, putting them back inside, and closing the doors, making sure they had water and food.

Mentally he took inventory as he returned each dog, muttering under his breath as he wondered what kind of idiot would do this.

Once he got all the dogs inside their enclosures, he found that two were missing. Mitchell checked the back door and found it still bolted. He hoped they weren't outside in this weather. Maybe they had gotten out with whoever had done this. Mitchell was so damned angry he could spit quarters. Any of his dogs could have been hurt, or they could have fought. When he got his hands on whoever had done this, he would strangle the bastard.

Bowser and Muffy were missing. Muffy was a little Maltese mix and tended to be timid. He searched around and finally found her under his feeding worktable, quivering way back in the corner, the poor little thing. Mitchell managed to coax her out with some food and gently petted her, trying to calm her down. Part of him said to just bring her into the house, but he reminded himself how easily he could get himself involved with each of his dogs. He held her to his chest and closed his eyes, just standing still until she settled down. Then he put her in her enclosure, gave her some kibble as a treat, and closed the door. Now he needed to find Bowser, but he had no luck. No matter where he looked, the Bassett hound mix was nowhere to be found. He shouldn't be that hard to find, but Bowser was old and half deaf, so it was likely he wouldn't hear Mitchell calling for him.

Panic started to take hold, and he opened the door and peering out into the rain. "Bowser!" he called as loudly as he could, looking for any kind of movement. Nothing. He closed the door again and went through the entire barn, opening all the doors and checking under the tables once more.

"There you are," he said when he spied a tail sticking out from behind a vertical stack of the two-by-fours he used to make the enclosures. Bowser had tried to crawl behind them but left his tail sticking out. Relief washed through him as he got Bowser out and lifted the senior citizen back into his blanket-lined home and closed the door.

Mitchell left the barn, watching all around to try to see if anyone was about. He was still pissed as hell that someone had let all the dogs out, but at least whoever it was hadn't left the main door open so they could all get away into the stormy night. He could just imagine trying to round up a pack of scared, wet dogs in the dark. "You asshole. Whoever is doing this, you could have hurt my dogs, and I'll get you for that," he called against the downpour as he made his way back toward the house.

"What happened?" Beau asked. "I was about to call out the cavalry." He set his phone on the table and returned to feeding Jessica.

Mitchell shivered and set the shaken-out umbrella near the door. "Our visitor was back. The shed door was open, and someone let all the dogs out inside the barn. They were barking up a storm, and I found them all through the shelter. Thank God none of them had gotten outdoors." He wanted to scream. "Whoever is doing this shit has a lot to answer for. Those dogs could have hurt themselves or each other." He wondered if he should call the police. Maybe they could help, but any clues to who it could be would probably have washed away, and Mitchell had touched everything trying to get the dogs back where they belonged.

"You mean that someone was out there on a night like this?" Beau's eyes widened and nerves built up behind them.

"I guess." Now it was his turn to not want to be alone. It was hard enough knowing that someone was after Beau… and now this. If it were just Beau, then they had a good idea who might be behind it, but with someone after him, Mitchell was clueless.

"Has anyone been angry with you?"

Mitchell shrugged. "I had a client whose old dog died today. He was angry and yelled at me before storming off." He really didn't want to think that Alan was behind this, but he couldn't write it off. Though he somehow doubted that Alan was behind whoever was watching them. Maybe there were multiple things going on. God, he wished he knew what was behind all this.

"Okay. But would he do something like this?"

"I don't want to think so. He was hurting because he lost his dog. I don't think he'd let all my animals loose." He sighed as he thought. "There's one thing that bothers me. If someone really wanted to hurt me, they'd have let the dogs out of the building." He nodded as the events of the evening became clearer. "This was someone sending a message. That they could get to me when they want to. I had no idea anything was wrong until the pizza guy mentioned the open door."

Speaking of pizza, Mitchell took the one that had been delivered into the kitchen and placed it in the oven to warm it up. Then he got plates and a couple of beers, which he brought into the living room.

"I didn't mean to be gone that long and leave you hungry." He rubbed Jessica's back and then leaned down. Beau kissed him and then slipped his hand around the back of Mitchell's neck, deepening the kiss.

Mitchell pulled away breathlessly and returned to the kitchen to get the pizza. He needed a few seconds to clear his head because all he wanted was to put Jessica to bed and spend the next few hours ravishing Beau, food be damned.

The physical part of a relationship was easy. That was the part that he could do, and it didn't bother him. What did was the rest of it, especially trust. Mitchell wanted to be able to trust Beau, but he was having difficulty. Even as he was putting the dogs back in their cages, the notion that Beau might have done this had flashed across his mind. Luke used to do things like that. He'd create some crisis and then swoop in to solve it to make himself seem indispensable and to make Mitchell more dependent on him. It had taken a long time for Mitchell to cotton on to that.

The more he thought about it, the more he was sure that Beau had had nothing to do with letting the dogs loose. What was he going to do, do all that while carrying Jessica around? It was crazy, and yet the idea wasn't rational—the fear and hurt weren't rational. That was the problem. Mitchell wanted Beau to trust him, and yet he was ashamed to admit, even to himself, that he wasn't willing to give the same level of trust that he hoped for from others and especially Beau.

Mitchell got the pizza out of the oven, carried it and a potholder to the living room, and placed them on the table. "Help yourself. I didn't get one with too many toppings." Mitchell realized he hadn't even asked Beau what he liked on pizza, but it didn't seem to matter. Beau took two slices and ate while Jessica played on a blanket on the floor.

Beau kept glancing at him, and Mitchell tried to act normally, but he felt guilty as hell. Luke had been gone for years, and he should have been smart enough to be able to move past all this. Instead, a ghost from his past had reared up and seemed ever-present in his current chance at a relationship. "Were all the dogs okay?" Beau was likely just trying to make conversation.

"Yes. I had to find two of them where they'd hidden, and they were scared but fine." He took a bite of his pizza. It was a little dry from being reheated, but still pretty good. He turned on the television to fill the vacuum, and they settled back to watch a baking competition. Not that Mitchell had much interest in baking, but he did love eating, and the cakes and stuff always looked pretty yummy.

"I think I should take Jessica home," Beau said after they had finished the entire pizza. "The rain seems to have let up, and I need to get her to bed."

Mitchell didn't want them to leave. He was nervous about being home alone with someone watching him. But Beau was in the same boat. They had both had someone hanging around them, making threatening gestures. Mitchell figured they were safer together, but he wasn't sure how he could ask Beau to stay. He had come over to check on him and obviously wasn't prepared to spend the night. Jessica required supplies, and all of that stuff was back at Beau's. Not to mention the fact that Randi was still there. "Are you going to be okay?" he asked Beau.

"I think I have to be." Beau slowly got to his feet. "I know something is going on. I wish I knew what it was." He sighed. "I think I'm going to call Gerome and confront him about it. I'm tired of being frightened and worried all the time." His words seemed bold, but Mitchell could sense the worry inside.

"I think that's a good idea," he agreed. "Maybe he'll let something slip about his recent activities. If he is behind what's been going on, then we need to know about it."

Beau nodded. "I can't bury my head in the sand and wait for the next thing to happen. If I can uncover what's going on, then we can figure out how to stay safe."

Mitchell liked that Beau used the word *we*. "Do you want me to come with you?" he offered.

Beau seemed to ponder the idea. "You don't have to. I…." He lifted his gaze from Jessica. "Look, I've been a royal pain in the butt to you even before we met. You've watched over us and even gave up your dog so we can feel safer and not be alone. I can't ask you to do more for us."

Mitchell drew closer to where Beau stood holding Jessica. "You didn't ask," he whispered, gently stroking little Jessica's soft hair as he tried to explain how he felt. The words were there, on the tip of his tongue, but he couldn't bring himself to say them. He wished he knew why, but they refused to come out. "You go ahead and get this little sweetheart home, and I'll take care of things here before following you over. Then, if you want, I'll be with you when you call Gerome."

He hoped to hell they got some answers. Mitchell really thought that Gerome was behind all this, even the things at his place. If Gerome was watching Beau, then he had figured out that Mitchell and Beau were getting close, and maybe he wasn't too happy about it. It made sense to Mitchell. In his mind all they needed to do was prove it and they could put an end to whatever Gerome was trying to pull. But first they had to get him dead to rights, and Beau's idea of confronting him sounded like the best opening salvo.

Chapter 10

GOOD GOD, he wanted Mitchell to come home with him and never leave. There was definitely someone out there, and it appeared they were after both of them. It seemed to Beau that Mitchell thought Gerome was behind all this. Beau wasn't so sure. He had to do something to try to figure all this out, but he was a program director for a college, not a sleuth.

Once he got home, with Mitchell in his car behind him, he parked close to the house, covered Jessica with a blanket to keep the rain off her, loaded himself up, and hurried to the house, where Randi jumped and pranced to greet them. Her tail wagged a mile a minute. As soon as Beau set Jessica down and pulled away the blanket, Randi stuck her nose inside the carrier, sniffing and for all the world looking like she was checking out *her* baby.

"That dog is obsessed," Mitchell said as he took off his wet jacket. The muscles on his arms and shoulders bunched with the simple movement. Beau loved the way Mitchell moved, gracefully, as though each movement were practiced and intended to drive him crazy. His hand shook, and Beau lifted his gaze to Mitchell's eyes, which were wide, pupils dilated. In that second, he realized that Mitchell was just as scared as he was. "What the hell is going on?" He swallowed hard and continued holding his dripping jacket. "I was thinking that I should check your shed before we go any further. See if anyone has been in there lately."

Beau nodded and handed him an umbrella. "I'll put on all the outside lights." It was all he could think of to do. "I'd go with you…."

Mitchell shook his head and set down his jacket and the umbrella before coming closer. "You take care of Jessica and keep your phone close. I'll be gone just a few minutes, and if I'm not back soon or if you hear or see anything, call the police right away." Mitchell drew him in, hugging and then kissing him hard.

"You aren't going off to war," he teased before returning Mitchell's kiss with enough force for just that occasion. His heart beat faster, and he didn't want to let Mitchell go. Having him in his arms felt so right. The world outside his door could go screw itself for all he cared. What mattered was right here and right now. At least it was in that moment.

Randi gave a small bark, and Beau smiled, pulling back. "I'll have my phone, but don't you dare be gone long. I'm going to get Jessica changed, and then after we make a phone call, I intend to put you to bed… early." Beau felt as though he were growling.

He wanted all the rest of this intrigue to go away so he could have some quiet time with Mitchell without worrying about ex-husbands, being stalked, or people trying to hurt their dogs. It made him angry and got his nerves working overtime. What had he done to deserve this? What had either of them done?

"I'll be right back," Mitchell said.

Beau nodded, biting his lower lip. "I'm going to get her changed, but I'll have my phone." He sat near Jessica's carrier, lifted her out, and shared a smile with his daughter. He placed his phone right in front of him on the coffee table. "I'm giving you no more than ten minutes." Beau checked the time on the phone as Mitchell pulled on his jacket and left the house with the umbrella.

Beau never saw ten minutes crawl by so slowly. He tried to coax some smiles out of Jessica, but his heart wasn't in it. He transferred her to his shoulder and began walking the room, checking out the windows, but he neither heard nor saw anything other than rain. Even the outside lights didn't penetrate very far.

Beau let the curtains fall back into place and then checked the time once again. The ten minutes had passed. He reached for the phone just as the front door opened and Mitchell stepped inside.

"Everything looked the same," he said as he pulled off the sopping-wet jacket. "I checked around outside as well. With the rain it was impossible to tell, but the inside of the shed hasn't been disturbed."

"That's a relief, at least. I need to put Jessica to bed, and then I'm going to call Gerome. There's some beer and things in the refrigerator. Help yourself. I'll be back as quickly as I can."

He went down to the bathroom and got the bathing things ready for Jessica. He made sure it was the right temperature and undressed her, placed her in her tiny plastic bathtub, and gently washed her. Jessica fussed—she didn't like a bath—but he got her clean and wrapped her in a warm, fluffy pink towel. Now that she was toasty warm, she quieted. Beau got her into a diaper and a sleeper with a happy worm on it and rocked her to sleep with a bottle.

"You sing beautifully," Mitchell whispered just as Beau finished a lullaby his mother used to sing. He didn't remember the words, so he hummed the tune, and it rarely failed to settle Jessica to sleep.

Beau slowly got up and motioned his head toward the chair. Mitchell sat down, and Beau passed Jessica into his arms. He stepped back as she settled, looking up at Mitchell, who lowered his gaze to hers. Beau watched them, leaning against the doorframe.

"You're a pretty girl," Mitchell whispered to Jessica, who was tired, her eyes slowly closing. Mitchell rocked and hummed to her in his deep voice. He was a little off-key, but Jessica didn't seem to mind. Jessica settled into sleep, and Mitchell raised his face. Beau might have seen the tracks of a tear on his cheek. He wasn't sure.

Mitchell got up and approached the crib. Beau took the empty bottle, and Mitchell placed Jessica in the crib. Randi came in and settled on the seat of the chair where she could see Jessica, then curled up to sleep as well. Beau still wasn't wild about Randi sleeping in Jessica's room, but he didn't want to keep her door closed, so Randi would just come in anyway. He was pretty sure she couldn't get into the crib itself. "She could steal my heart," Mitchell said from the doorway as he left the room.

"How long had you been watching?" Beau asked as he closed the door partway.

"Long enough," Mitchell said quietly. "I never thought I wanted children." He stepped away, and they headed for the living room.

"It's a huge responsibility, but I can't see myself any other way right now."

"I get that." Mitchell sat on the sofa with Beau next to him.

"Can I ask you something?" Beau asked. Mitchell nodded his response. "Do you want a family?"

"Yes," Mitchell responded. "I do. I didn't always know that was what I wanted. There has been so much change in the past few weeks that it's sometimes hard to know what will make me happy and what won't." He sighed and kept himself hunched up and closed off.

"Is the whole family thing part of the reason you like me… and Jessica?" Beau had been thinking about that lately, and he needed to know.

Mitchell sat up straighter and leaned closer. "Of course not. I think Jessica is the sweetest, cutest, best baby I could imagine. When I hold her and she looks up at me with those big trusting eyes, my belly feels like Jell-O and I wonder how I can possibly be good enough for you… and for her."

Beau titled his head slightly to the side. "Why do you think that?"

Mitchell shifted nervously, drawing in on himself once again. "It's hard to explain or admit, but I spent the last five years guarding myself from everything. The only way I could open my heart was to the dogs and pets I treat. Other than that, I shut myself off from everything." He finally sat back. "Why would anyone want someone like me in their life?" Mitchell sighed and seemed to grow smaller by the second.

"And you cut yourself off because of Luke?" Beau asked.

"Yeah. After all this time I thought I was over him, but now that I've met you and Jessica, Luke seems to be looking over my shoulder. I can feel the old doubts and concerns sitting on top of me. I spent years in therapy. I built my own life, one that I love, and I thought I had it all. Then I meet my hunky neighbor, and all the things I thought I knew are out the window."

Beau grinned. "First thing, I'm glad you think I'm hunky, and I'm relieved that there isn't some off-the-wall dynamic behind your interest in me." He took Mitchell's hand. "As for being messed up and worried, you think I'm not?" He rolled his eyes. "I'm just as worried and have the same kind of shadow over me that you do." He shrugged. "And if you're looking for answers, I sure as hell don't have them. But I did find someone who's more important than my worries and who needs my care. It doesn't matter to Jessica what Gerome did to me. She needs my attention and my love. That has to be my top priority. I can't let Gerome or anyone else take that number-one spot. She has to come first." He squeezed Mitchell's hand. "And I saw the gentleness in you too."

Mitchell lifted his gaze. "Huh? How…?" The stutter was kind of cute.

"I saw that same care and trust in you while she was in your arms. You were relaxed and focused on her. It was like an hour of yoga wrapped into fifteen minutes. The lines on your face smoothed out and you just looked at her like she was the earth and stars." Beau reached for his phone. "I know you care for her. I…." It was his turn to be nervous. "I can't help wondering if you're here because of her or because of me?" He swallowed hard. "I know you like me, but…."

Mitchell grinned and drew closer. "I like Jessica. She's adorable. But it seems her daddy has done something no one else could do. He touched my cynical, hardened heart and warmed it. I don't know if anyone else could possibly have done that." Mitchell kissed him, and the heat built in seconds. "So to answer your question, it isn't just Jessica. I care for her, but I think I'm falling for her daddy."

"And it terrifies you," Beau said, reading the look in Mitchell's eyes.

He nodded. "I guess it does. But being with you is worth a little worry and maybe a touch of emotional terror. I know you aren't going to hit me the way Luke did. But it's hard to open myself up again. Yet I know that if I don't, I'll never have the things I really want." He swallowed hard, his breath tickling Beau's lips.

Mitchell wanted him, and what Mitchell said touched Beau's heart. He understood reluctance and the fear of being hurt. But the truth was that no matter what Mitchell said, Beau had more to lose. He had to think of Jessica as well as himself. She already liked Mitchell, that was clear, but what if things didn't work out and Mitchell just left? Yes, it would hurt him, but Jessica couldn't say when she was hurt. "You're not the only one with something to lose and a heart to protect." Hell, he had two to watch out for. His mind began to shift gears. "I need to make that call."

Mitchell nodded and stayed where he was, and Beau picked up the phone and dialed the familiar number.

"Yeah, what do you want?" Gerome snapped.

"Is that how you answer the phone?" Beau asked.

"I was working and really in the zone. You know how hard it will be to get used to a new workspace, so I'm really pushing it right now," he griped. "But I did it. I found another studio. The only place I could afford is well out of the city, but it comes with a room for me, so I can make it work." Beau heard him setting down his tools. "I hope you're happy."

Beau pursed his lips. "I'm not happy about any of this, and I certainly wasn't thrilled with being hit and then made to feel like it was my fault. You're the one with control and anger-management issues. If you want to blame someone for what's happened, take a long, hard look into the fucking mirror, Gerome. You brought this on yourself." He took a deep breath, because damn, that felt really good to say. "This is no one's fault but your own, and any excuses you have, I don't want to hear."

"I guess I got a little crazy for a while. I wasn't working, and I spent a lot of time there following you around, hoping I could convince you to take me back."

Beau met Mitchell's gaze. "What did you do?"

"I spent a lot of time seeing who you were seeing, watching. And yeah, I followed you to a few places. I kept hoping that I could get some time alone with you and convince you that I wasn't such a bad guy and that you and I should try again." A clang sounded from behind Gerome, followed by a soft, deep voice.

"Is someone there? Did I interrupt something?" Beau smirked, wondering if he'd interrupted a hook-up of some kind. Gerome had been pretty wild before they met. It wouldn't surprise him if Gerome returned to old habits.

"No. I was working, and I have a model in the studio. He's getting ready to go." Gerome turned away from the phone to say goodbye. "Anyway, the house in the city will be empty in a few days, and you can put it on the market. It should sell quickly, and I'll come in and sign any papers when you need me to."

This was so much easier than Beau could possibly have imagined. He shared a look with Mitchell, wondering what the hell was going on and if Gerome was trying to put him on somehow.

"Okay. Thank you." He shrugged and wondered what the fuck. Gerome never gave up on anything easily. He usually pushed and prodded until he got what he wanted.

"I need to work so I can finish this piece before I have to move." Gerome seemed in a hurry.

"Okay. Let me know when you're out and I'll take it from there." Maybe this was going to work out well after all. The house would be sold, and the last thing that tied the two of them together would be gone. "I'll talk to you later." He was about to hang up.

"Yeah. Oh… and I wanted to tell you that your dog is really cute." Gerome hung up, and a chill ran up Beau's spine. He set his phone down and tried to make sense of the call.

"Well. How did it go? Do you think he's behind all this?" Mitchell asked.

Beau shrugged, staring at the wall behind Mitchell. "I don't think so. He's moving on and found a place. I can put the house and studio on the market next week. It was too good to be true. But then he talked about Randi. Gerome hates dogs." He lifted his gaze. "I think that might have been his way of trying to scare me."

"How?"

"The remark sounded innocent enough, but she was the point of the attack. Someone tried to hurt her, and they let your dogs out." He tried to think, but his mind whirled with fear.

"You really think it could have been him?" Mitchell asked.

Beau nodded slowly. "It's possible. I know he was in Philadelphia because I heard him setting his tools aside. He always uses this old reclaimed metal table in the studio, and I heard the metal clanking down on it. From what he said, I'd like to think that whatever has gotten into him is past. He's moving on, and so am I. But I just don't know if he tried to poison Randi." He attempted to get comfortable and failed completely. "Gerome was pretty angry before…." Beau needed to get his head around this. "If he had just ended the call, I probably would have thought that everything was okay, but he had to throw in that last jibe, just to be sure."

Mitchell scooted right next to him. "So you think that was him telling you he did it?"

"Or that he truly has been watching and he just wanted me to know that he saw me and us together. I have no idea what's going on in his head." Beau shivered and then sighed. "At least we know he isn't here right now. Maybe with the house being sold, we can both move on and things will quiet down." His one consolation was that if Gerome had been behind the watching and the attacks, then maybe it was over. Only time would tell.

"We need to call Red," Mitchell said, already pulling out his phone.

"Yeah, we should." Just like before, there wasn't a lot he could do to help them, but at least he might have some insight. Mitchell made the call and put the phone on speaker. He explained what he had found.

Red was clearly cautious. "Look, it sounds as though this guy is escalating. First you think he was hanging around, and then an attempt was made on Beau's dog. Now all of Mitchell's dogs were let loose." He hummed to himself. "I'd sure like to know what this person thinks they're going to get out of this."

"Us too," Beau said. "I keep thinking that we're being toyed with. Like this is some sort of game to them and we're stuck wondering what the rules are."

"It's possible. Was anything tampered with?" Red asked. "What bothers me is why the dogs were let loose but the main doors weren't opened. That would have made one hell of a mess and created chaos for you."

"I wondered that too," Mitchell agreed. "It's strange, but at the time all I could think about was getting the dogs back inside their cages, swearing under my breath because they could have fought and hurt each other. We're keeping an eye out, but I don't know what we're going to do. If this guy is escalating like you said, then I keep wondering what's going to come next."

That was the really frightening part.

IT TOOK Beau a little while before his mind would move on from Gerome and his riddles. Mitchell turned on the television, keeping the volume low so they didn't wake Jessica. "I have Netflix," Beau said when they didn't find anything to watch. Mitchell switched over, and they found an original movie about a vet and elephants.

"I love animal stories," Mitchell said as he settled back, putting an arm around Beau, drawing him closer. "Sometimes I think that I love animals more than people."

Beau rolled his eyes and snorted. "Duh. You have a dozen or so dogs that you're trying to find homes for and you spend all your time either at the clinic or at the shelter. You'd have to love animals."

A sharp bark came from Jessica's bedroom, followed by another. Mitchell jumped up and raced forward.

"She must see something," Beau said.

"No." Mitchell didn't stop for a second. "That's distress." He reached Jessica's door and hurried inside. By the time Beau arrived, Mitchell had a crying Jessica in his arms, and he rocked her gently, looking her over. Randi raced around their legs and barked again before jumping back into the chair.

"What is it?"

"She spit up and choked," Mitchell said. Jessica was already calming, oblivious to the danger. Mitchell passed her to Beau, and he cuddled his daughter, heart racing a mile a minute as he looked her over from head to foot. "She seems okay, and it mustn't have been for very long. As soon as I picked her up, she gasped for air and started crying." Mitchell sounded panicked.

Beau did his best to calm Jessica as well as himself. "It's okay," he soothed as he rocked her in his arms, unsure what to do. "She seems okay." He checked her face, which was pink and had normal color. "I think we got here in time."

Mitchell picked up Randi and stroked her. "You were a good dog. You alerted us to the bad stuff." He continued stroking down her back. "Yes, you are. You're the best baby watchdog there's ever been."

Beau's mind raced with possibilities, and eventually he got Jessica a fresh sleeper and put her in it, making sure she was warm enough before gently rocking her to sleep and putting her into the crib. Then he too praised Randi. Mitchell placed Randi back on her chair, and she settled into position as they left the room.

"I thought my heart was going to stop," Beau whimpered as he went to the kitchen for a drink of water. The fear was still fresh. He took a drink before going back to peer into Jessica's room. Everything was exactly as he left it, with Jessica asleep and Randi watching from her chair. Mitchell slid his arms around his waist. "I'm so scared." He turned around slowly. "I keep worrying that if I do something wrong, I'm going to hurt her and…." Beau put his arms around Mitchell's neck, buried his face in his shoulder, and cried. The hurt and fear were damn near overwhelming and needed to come out.

Jessica was his child, his daughter, and the thought of losing her for any reason was enough to scare the living daylights out of him. "It's okay," Mitchell said, holding him and just letting him see this through. Part of Beau was ashamed of himself for breaking down like this, but it was too much.

"No, it's not. She could have been hurt… or worse." Beau wiped his eyes. "I can't lose her. I just can't."

"I know."

"And then I think about Franklin and Helen. I called the attorney that I used in Philadelphia, and they didn't think I had anything to worry about. They have no relationship with Jessica, and since their son signed away his rights, it pretty much signed away theirs as well. The attorney said they could visit if I allowed it, but Amy's will was very clear that I was to raise her, and it's her wishes that are paramount." He swallowed hard. "But they could still sue and drag me through months of hell if they wanted to. I saw the ring she was wearing—they have money, and plenty of it." Beau was getting overwhelmed and he knew it, but the worries and fears of the past few weeks had built on one another, and now they were all coming out at once.

"First, we'll take things as they come. Secondly, we got to Jessica in time and she's fine. You can check on her more often if you like, but what happened was a fluke." Beau hated that he might have made Mitchell feel guilty. In his heart he knew what happened had been an accident and that Jessica was okay.

"I know it was." The thing was that Beau was afraid and didn't know what to do to prevent something like that from happening again. "It's just everything at once. It all seems out of my control, and I hate shit like that." He took a deep breath to calm his nerves and tried to get his mind to settle on what was important. Jessica was fine and sound asleep once again. Everything was going to be okay. All he needed to do was remain calm.

"Come on." Mitchell moved away and left the room. Beau heard the television switch off along with the lights before he rejoined him. "You need to rest so you can think straight. You're overwhelmed and tired." He pushed open the bedroom door, and Beau went inside. Mitchell followed him, and Beau got undressed like an automaton. He was trying not to think of the consequences, of what might have happened if they hadn't gotten there in time, if Randi hadn't raised the alarm. He was lucky. He needed to figure out how to prevent that in the future.

Beau got into bed, snuggling next to Mitchell. Beau hoped that Mitchell wasn't disappointed that he couldn't do anything else, but his mind was on Jessica and how he had almost lost her. Beau yawned and then got out of bed and crossed the hall to peer into Jessica's room.

She was still asleep and as perfect as ever. Mitchell pressed to his back, his warmth welcome in the coolness of the hallway. He didn't say anything, standing along with him until he guided Beau back to the bedroom and they got under the covers. Eventually Beau fell asleep.

"SO THIS is where you got to," Mitchell said the following morning, standing in the doorway of

Jessica's room. She was still in Beau's arms as he sat in the rocking chair, Randi lying at his feet. The little dog's tail wagged and she stretched and headed to Mitchell, looking up at him with her huge eyes. "I get it. You're Jessica's dog until it's time to eat, and then you'll give puppy-dog eyes to anyone who'll feed you." Mitchell scooped her up with a sigh. "Come on, then, I'll feed you." He rolled his eyes as he stroked her head. Beau watched Mitchell's boxer-shorts-covered butt as he turned.

The man was sexy as hell, and Beau smiled at the thought that Mitchell actually liked him. He listened as Mitchell moved through the house, and then his footsteps got closer until he entered the room and carefully took Jessica from Beau's arms. He placed her back in the crib, and she barely stirred.

"What time is it?" Beau asked.

"Just after five," Mitchell whispered and led him back to bed. "Your back is going to hate you for spending hours in that chair." He pulled back the covers, and Beau slipped under them, closing his eyes. He was nearly asleep when Mitchell got in as well and tugged him right to him, slipping a warm hand over his belly. Beau was instantly aroused. He slowly rolled over, kissing Mitchell as he slid his hands down his back and under the elastic of his boxers, then over his butt, pressing their hips closer together. There were many things he wanted to say, but at the moment with Mitchell kissing him and his hands working their magic, all Beau wanted was to get lost in the sensation of being cared for.

"That's it," Mitchell whispered, gently pushing the fabric past Beau's hips. "Show me what you need."

Beau groaned under his breath. He didn't want to make a sound in case they woke Jessica and the sexiness bubble that formed around them burst. He needed this, and he pressed himself to Mitchell, then tugged him back until he climbed on top, Mitchell's weight pressing him into the mattress, solid and firm, weighty and perfect, reassuring him when things seemed to get out of control. "I'm just all churned up right now."

Mitchell gazed into his eyes. "I know." He leaned forward, capturing Beau's lips, and Beau's belly calmed and the nerves that had been playing the piano across his spine for hours instantly settled. Beau put his arms around Mitchell's neck and held on as he kissed him deep, hard, damn near possessively. God, he loved that. "Just relax and look into my eyes." Mitchell smoothed his hand over Beau's cheek. "I know you're worried and frazzled, but everything is going to be okay." He kissed Beau again, and more of the worry slipped away.

Mitchell shimmied off his boxers until they were skin to skin. He pushed away the covers and sat back. Beau felt bare and exposed for a few seconds until Mitchell smiled and ran his hands down his chest. "Why are you worried?"

Beau shrugged. "I guess I never thought of myself as sexy." He swallowed hard. "I was surprised when… my ex….” He wasn't going to say his name. “Showed an interest in me. I mean, I….”

“Bullshit.” Mitchell grinned. “I'm calling BS on that. You're hot. I knew that the second I saw you.” Beau was about to argue when Mitchell sucked at the base of his neck, and he growled, stretching to give him better access because… damn. Tingles ran down his spine. “You need to not listen to anything that idiot said.”

“You've never met him.” Beau shivered and held Mitchell tighter. He never wanted this to end.

“Yeah, but he hurt you and let you get away. That makes him an idiot.” Mitchell hovered over him, his breath tickling his belly. “You know we have much better things to do and talk about other than idiots.” Mitchell grinned and slipped his fingers around the base of Beau's cock, punctuating his words with warm, wet heat that sent Beau into the stratosphere.

“Mitchell… I….” He inhaled sharply, his eyes rolling as Mitchell sucked him hard. Everything seemed to narrow to just the two of them until Randi decided she was going to join them.

Mitchell pulled away, growling deeply. Randi took one look at him, turned around, and raced out of the room.

“Smart dog.”

“Now, where was I?” Mitchell asked before sliding his lips down Beau's cock once again, instantly sending him on a trajectory toward the moon. Beau closed his eyes, letting Mitchell guide their pleasure.

"Oh yeah," Beau breathed, and Mitchell's groan rumbled in his throat around his cock. "Jesus…." His head pounded, and Beau lay still, soaking in the attention and care like a sponge.

"I know what you need." Mitchell continued his ministrations, driving Beau higher and higher. He tried not to think of anything else as their passion built. Beau wondered how much longer he was going to be able to control himself. His hands shook and his legs vibrated on the bed. He closed his eyes, trying to think of something to hold off his climax for just a little longer. This was too amazing and mind-blowing for it to be over already. He clamped his eyes closed because even though all he wanted was to watch Mitchell take him and see his cock disappearing between Mitchell's amazing lips, he…. Fuck, just that thought was enough to send a spike of desire running through him that he was barely able to control.

When Mitchell pulled back, leaving Beau just this side of the point of no return, Beau panted and sighed, arms splayed beside him, a moan escaping his lips before he could stop it. "Oh God." Beau lay still, and Mitchell gathered him into his arms and pressed Beau against the mattress. "I promise I won't hurt you."

Beau nodded. "I know that." He tugged Mitchell down into a kiss and rolled them on the bed. Now he had Mitchell at his mercy.

"What are you going to do with me?" Mitchell said, closing his arms around Beau's back, snaking his hands downward until they cupped Beau's butt. Beau wriggled a little and pressed their lips together, tasting Mitchell and pressing his tongue between his lips until they parted slightly. Beau loved the taste of Mitchell on his tongue, and he wanted more. Beau wanted it all. Pulling back, he slid down Mitchell's sleek, hard body, tracing the lines of his chest and belly muscles with his tongue, gathering small moans and whimpers like spring flowers with the prize, Mitchell's cock, long and thick, stretched out against his belly.

Beau slid his lips around the pink head and then slowly down the shaft, loving the musky smell and rich taste that burst in his mouth as Mitchell's cock slid over his tongue. He wanted to give Mitchell as much pleasure as he had been given, and he took him deep, Mitchell's belly muscles quivering under Beau's hand. "Beau… I…."

The warning was enough for Beau to back away. "I want you, Mitchell. Is that okay?" Mitchell hesitated, and Beau felt that familiar intrusive presence sliding into the room with them. "I understand."

Mitchell cupped his cheeks, cradling Beau's face. "I haven't done that since before… well…. I've always topped because I needed to stay in control. Not that there's been much of anything like that in a long time. But…."

Beau placed his hands on top of Mitchell's. "I fully understand. And we don't have to do anything that you aren't ready for—that neither of us is." He pulled Mitchell's hands way, still holding them, and kissed the back of one. “There are plenty of other ways that we can show one another what we feel.”

Mitchell smiled all the way to his eyes. “Is that your way of saying that we’re making love?” He swallowed hard, and Beau nodded. It was the closest that he could come to saying the L-word right now. Things seemed to be happening quickly, even though they had agreed to go slowly. Not that he regretted a moment with Mitchell. “Then yes. I want to show you how I feel.” Mitchell moved his arms around Beau and held him in a fierce embrace. “I don’t ever want anything to happen to you.” The shakiness in his voice left Beau curious. It was at odds with the conviction in his eyes.

“I know how you feel.” He buried his face in Mitchell’s neck, inhaling deeply as he lost part of himself in Mitchell. He’d been afraid he would never be able to do that again, and yet as Mitchell rocked slowly back and forth, Beau sank into whatever was happening between the two of them, letting it wash over him. All too soon, he was on a knife-edge, feeling Mitchell against him, tasting him in their kiss, inhaling his scent, and damned if the whimpers from deep in Mitchell’s throat didn’t work to send him higher until Beau felt like he was flying and never wanted to come back down to earth. With a cry, the flood inside him burst forth and Beau shot as high as the clouds, wishing he could stay forever.

FOR THE time he was with Mitchell, Beau could let go of his worries and fears. At least it didn’t feel like

Gerome was right there with him. He dared to hope that the specter of his marriage was finally receding into the past and he could move on. His mind floated, and Mitchell was right there with him, holding and comforting him, slowly petting up and down his back until Beau returned to himself. Sometimes he loved that feeling so much he wished he would never come down.

A thump from outside made both of them still. Jessica cried, and Beau got out of bed and grabbed something to put on while Mitchell did the same, then hurried away and out through the house. Beau changed Jessica and got her a bottle. He walked her as she sucked down the bottle like she was starving. It was still early, and he hoped she might go back to sleep, but Jessica was obviously wide awake. Beau continually listened for any noise from outside as he fed her, peering out the side of the curtains to see what was going on.

"It was one of the trash cans. The wind has come up," Mitchell said. He grabbed the door before the wind blew it off the hinges. "I hate to leave you, but I need to get dressed and check on the dogs. They are going to be hungry, and with this wind, they're going to be anxious. Are you going to be okay here?"

Beau nodded. "We'll be fine. Do you have clinic hours today?"

"Yes. I'll get the dogs set. I have someone who will come in at nine or so and see that all the dogs get a good walk." He yawned. "I also have to catch up on a bunch of paperwork. There's a festival in

Boiling Springs this weekend that I want to get ready for. I was thinking of taking some of the dogs down for an adoption booth. Maybe you and Jessica would want to stop by."

"I'd like that," Beau said. Mitchell tended to throw his whole self into everything he did—the clinic, the dogs, helping Beau. He never seemed to stop. Mitchell hurried back to the bedroom and emerged dressed in the clothes from the day before. Beau kissed him, and then Mitchell raced out the door, going a million miles a minute. Beau yawned and checked that all the doors were closed and locked as the wind continued to pound against the side of the house.

Jessica fussed a little, and Beau did his best to soothe her. He wasn't ready to get up and would have liked a few more hours of sleep, but he buckled Jessica in her swing, which she seemed to love, and then made himself a quick breakfast before attempting to do some work of his own. Even though Jessica was there with him and Randi kept them both company, it surprised Beau just how empty the house felt without Mitchell. He had so easily become a part of their lives. Beau couldn't help wondering if it all wasn't too good to be true. After all, Gerome certainly had been. Was he a fool for dipping his feet into relationship waters so soon after getting away from Gerome? Beau really wished he had the answer.

Chapter 11

MITCHELL MANAGED to make it to the clinic on time for his ten o'clock opening. As he'd expected, the dogs were riled up and full of energy. Jeremy arrived exactly on time, and he put some dogs in the run and got leads to walk the rest. He was a great kid, and with the way the dogs took to him, you'd think he was wearing hamburger underwear.

"Is everything okay?" Val asked when she came in. She put her things away and got situated at the front desk to welcome their first clients. "You look a little worse for wear."

"Jessica had a rough night," Mitchell explained.

Val nodded. "I see. You and Beau are getting pretty close." She smiled and practically clapped her hands together in excitement. "That young man is very special. Not all guys would so easily change their entire lives to take care of a child like that." She was correct, and Mitchell willed himself not to wonder how Luke would have reacted. Damn, now he was chastising himself for letting him intrude in his life once more.

"I know that's true." He tried not to let his own insecurities show, but Val was too quick.

"Okay, what's wrong?" They were the only two in the clinic at the moment. "What's gotten into your head?"

"Nothing important." He tried to pass his reaction off as nothing. He shouldn't have these worries. Beau had done nothing to remind him of Luke in any way, and yet Mitchell seemed to worry about him at every damn turn. Mitchell really wished he could figure out what it was that was getting to him so badly after all this time. He really should be past all this stuff.

"It is if you're worrying about it so much. Who is it that has you all tied in knots? Did Beau do something? Are you worried about dating someone with a child? You know a lot of men would find it intimidating to know that they will come in second behind a child. It's how it should be, but it's still hard to get some people to understand."

He stopped Val with a motion. "It isn't that. There has been someone hanging around. I've felt them there, and they tried to poison Randi, and they let all my dogs out. These things were no accident, and they have really gotten under my skin. Yeah, I know that someone is out there and they want something. I don't know what it is, but it's more than that. I get the feeling that there is something I'm missing. That somehow they're trying to send a message to Beau or me, and I just can't see it, and I should be able to."

"Look, I know there's some stuff going on, but don't let that come between you and what could be a very good thing. You're a good man who cares for everyone. Maybe it's time you let go of what's been holding you back and let someone else care for you. Because that's what we're talking about." Sometimes she saw so well it scared him. "This person from your past who did you so wrong… he's gone, and you need to let him die and stay in your past instead of affecting your present."

"I like Beau… a lot. But I picked the wrong person before and thought they were perfect for me. What if my judgment is whacked to hell?"

Val shook her head. "That shelter of yours is full of dogs that their owners thought weren't worth saving. You saw something different. That little Randi is the cutest thing, and you saved her life, just like you did for that three-legged dog and all those other ones. You haven't made a bad call yet when it comes to the pups, so let some of that confidence into the rest of your life." She patted his hand gently as though she were his grandmother and then straightened up and put on her professional face as the door opened with his first client.

Mitchell donned his white coat and took the patient back, a kitten who had gotten into something she shouldn't. The poor little thing howled and kept trying to cough up the bit of string that was caught in her throat. Mitchell got it out, and Mary, the eight-year-old owner, hugged the kitten gently.

"You need to be very careful. Little ones like this don't necessarily know what's food and what isn't." He didn't want to be mean.

"I'll be careful," Mary said, a little teary-eyed. "Aurora is going to be okay. Right?" She held the now-settled kitten in her arms.

"Yes. She'll be fine." Mitchell discussed the situation with her mother, and then they left, taking little Aurora with them. Mitchell wished that all his cases could be that easy.

THE REST of the day turned into one of those that Mitchell would just as soon forget. He stopped home at one point to check on his dogs and give them some attention and a few walks. They were fine. While he was there, he met with a prospective couple who adopted two dogs, one for each of them. They had been vacillating over email about which they wanted, and they compromised and took both. That was a bright spot in an otherwise dreary day that ended with him having to put two dogs and a cat to sleep. It was the only course of action, but it pained him every time he had to do it. At least none of the pets were alone when the time came. That was always a blessing.

"I'm glad that's over, and I hope it's a long time before something like that happens again," he told Bonnie as they disinfected the examination room and got things ready to close up for the night. It had been hard on her as well. Mitchell had gone into this line of work because of his love for animals and his drive to help them, but some days it seemed like he was helpless and could do nothing.

"Me too." She finished wiping down the table. "I'm almost done here, and Val is already gone. If you want to go on home and maybe spend some time with those doggie charges of yours, I'll close up for you and can check on the two we have in back before I turn in tonight."

"Thanks. I appreciate it." Mitchell took off his white coat, washed his hands well, and then made sure all the equipment was off and the money secured in the small safe. Then he left and got into his car. While he drove home, Beau called. "Hey, how was your day?"

"Wonderful, and the flowers are just beautiful. How did you know that I liked yellow roses? They're one of my favorites. I was thinking of planting some bushes along the one side of the house because I love them so much and… well… it was so thoughtful." Mitchell smiled for a second at Beau's happiness.

"Beau… I'm glad you think they're pretty, but I didn't send flowers." He pressed the accelerator a little harder, picking up speed. "Was there a card?"

"Yeah. It seemed a little enigmatic, but I thought you were just trying to be mysterious." Now Beau sounded concerned.

"Read it to me," Mitchell said, his heart beating faster by the second.

"Okay. It reads… 'Sweetheart, sometimes roses aren't red, but that doesn't mean that they don't carry as much care and warmth.'"

Mitchell felt the blood drain from his face. “And they were addressed to you?” Mitchell asked. “You’re sure of that?”

“What?” Beau asked. “You don’t think that someone could send me flowers?” He sounded hurt.

Mitchell didn’t blame him at all. “It’s not that. Tell me, are all the windows and doors closed and locked?” He was starting to panic. When Beau said they were, Mitchell asked him to call Red and gave him the number. “I need to check on the dogs to make sure they’re okay. Tell Red to come to your house, but if I’m not there in half an hour, send him to my place.” He forced air into his lungs.

“What’s going on? You’re scaring me.”

Mitchell was scaring himself, but if he was right, then they had been on the wrong track all along. “I need to check that everything is okay at the house, and then when I get there, I’ll explain everything to you and Red. Just do as I ask. I’ll get there just as soon as I possibly can.”

“Fine, but call me from the shelter so I know you’re okay.”

“I will.”

Mitchell ended the call and turned into his driveway. He pulled to a fast stop and got out of the car, listening for anything out of the ordinary. The dogs were barking, but with excitement, not worry. He peered inside the barn, and all seemed normal. Getting right to work, he changed out the runs to let other pups exercise and handed out treats, petting heads and getting plenty of licks and giving scratches.

There was a little Pekingese that had come in, and the poor thing just shook. Mitchell lifted him out of the cage and carried him in one arm while he worked to try to soothe the little guy. His owner had died and the family hadn't wanted him. Ruffy was probably mourning the loss and didn't know which way to turn. Mitchell fed him a few bits of kibble and finished up for the moment. He messaged Beau that he was okay, and after running from the barn at top speed, he slowly approached his house.

Everything seemed fine. The door was still locked, and when he stepped inside, nothing had been disturbed. He went from room to room, still holding Ruffy, who seemed more than happy to be carried and ate up the attention. Still, Mitchell checked out everything and peered in the back before locking up the house once again and bringing Ruffy with him to Beau's. The little guy soothed his jangled nerves.

Red was just arriving when he got there, and they both went inside. Randi approached Mitchell, tail wagging, and he set Ruffy down, prepared to pick him up again if they didn't get along. Randi sniffed Ruffy, and he did the same. They wagged their tails, and then Randi took off and Ruffy followed, barking once. Okay.

"What's going on?" Red asked.

"Jessica is asleep, so we need to talk quietly. I'm not really sure. I called Mitchell to thank him for the flowers, and he freaked."

Mitchell sat down next to Beau, with Red in the chair across from the sofa. "I checked everything at the shelter and the house before I came here."

"Why don't you tell us what's going on with these flowers?" Red said, indicating the bowl of gorgeous yellow roses.

"Okay. I didn't send them." He picked up the card, read it, and handed it to Red. "That sort of phrasing is exactly what Luke, my abusive ex, used to say to me. He used to hit me and was verbally abusive, and whenever he wanted to say he was sorry, he would send me yellow roses and write something like that. He hated red roses, so he always sent yellow." Mitchell tried to keep his thoughts from running in circles.

Red looked at the card front and back and then turned his attention to Mitchell. "Okay. That seems like a leap."

Mitchell shook his head. "It isn't. Believe me. I would know one of his cards and his handwriting anywhere. Those are from him. He wanted to send a message." Ice ran up and down Mitchell's back, and he shivered.

"Okay, let's assume that it is Luke who sent these flowers. Why would he do that?" Red asked.

Beau leaned forward. "When was the last time you saw him?" His voice calmed some of Mitchell's nerves. The dogs both hurried into the room. Randi jumped up onto the sofa. Ruffy simply stared at Mitchell, and he lifted him onto his lap and petted him slowly. Damn, he needed some puppy time right now.

"I last saw Luke maybe a few months after I left him. He had some other guy on his arm. We were in a bookstore, and I paid for my stuff as quickly as I could so I could leave. I figured he was with someone else, some other poor sap who had no idea the kind of guy he was dating… and then Luke was there next to me. He actually tried to get me to come back to him, saying he was sorry and that…." Mitchell really wished he didn't have to go over all this again. It had been five years. He had thought that Luke was out of his life for good. Now, fucking hell, the asshole was back, and he felt like the same fearful mess he had back then.

"What did you do?" Beau asked gently, resting a hand on his arm. "I know this sucks beyond belief. But just tell Red what happened."

Mitchell nodded. "I told Luke to go away and leave me alone. That I was done with him. He held my arm, and I yanked away and spoke more loudly, telling everyone in the store at the top of my voice that I wasn't a punching bag and that hitting people wasn't love. I was so angry, and it all came out. The guy Luke had come in with raced out of the store like a bat out of hell. Maybe Luke had already hit him and he'd seen the 'I'm sorry' routine. I don't know." He swallowed hard, his hand shaking. Beau took it, lacing their fingers together. "Anyway, I told him to get the hell away from me. And he left the store."

"And that was it?" Red asked.

Mitchell shook his head. "I left the bookstore after half an hour. I needed to calm down. Luke was waiting for me. He must have followed me. I was on my way to a friend's because it was his birthday, and the books I had were for him. He loved science fiction, and I had found some signed paperbacks. Luke caught me about two blocks from the bookstore and yanked me into a little walking tunnel between the buildings. He didn't say a word, but I knew he was going to let his fists do the talking. When he went to hit me, I fell to the ground, and he slugged a brick wall. Then I scampered away and ran like hell."

"Okay. If you think he's behind what's been happening, then give me some information." Red pulled out a pad. "What's his full name?"

"Luke Barrington. We met when I was in college at Michigan State. He's from Grayling, Michigan, and is my age, so he's thirty-four or thereabout. I don't remember his birthday." He wasn't happy Luke still took up any space in his head at all, but he felt a little blessed that he had forgotten some things about Luke.

"It's okay. That should be enough for me to track him down and see where he is now. Maybe he isn't even in this area of the country." Red asked some more questions, and Mitchell did his best to answer them.

"Why don't we just look him up on Facebook?" Beau offered and used his computer to bring up the people with that name. "Do any of these guys look like him?" Beau asked.

Mitchell got up and looked over his shoulder.

"Holy crap." Beau clicked on an icon, and a picture of Luke flashed on the screen. "That's the guy who delivered the flowers."

"What?" Mitchell queried. He had never thought to ask about the delivery person. Shit, Luke had been that close to Beau and Jessica.

"Are you sure?" Red asked.

Beau went through his posts, which were a strange mix of reposts and conspiracy theories. All the posts were recent, and the account had only been created a month ago.

"Yeah. That's him. He was only here a few hours ago. And look. That selfie was taken in downtown Carlisle. There's the old courthouse in the background. He has to be here. There's the proof." Beau started to shake, and Mitchell put an arm around him to try to comfort him. Beau patted his arm.

"Okay. So we know who's behind the things that have been happening here, and it's pretty safe to say that he's probably hanging around. I'm going to call the sheriff's office and report it. Pierre is a friend, and he'll be able to help. Technically this isn't my jurisdiction. It's the sheriff's department out here. I'll make sure this gets the attention it needs." Red went over all the details and copied the information from the Facebook page.

"What should we do?" Mitchell asked, growing concerned not just for himself but for Beau and Jessica. Luke wanted something from them as well, otherwise why deliver the flowers? He had been that near, which also meant he had wanted to see Beau up close. "Because so help me, if I get my hands on him, I'll kill him. If he so much as looks Beau or Jessica funny—hell, if he shows up again on my property.... I have a gun and I'll use it." Mitchell wasn't going to take chances.

"Okay, hold up, Sure Shot. Let me work with the sheriff's department to see if we can find him. So far we can't prove he's done anything wrong. All we know is that he delivered flowers to Beau. The stuff with Randi and the shelter, as well as the other suspicions, are just supposition. So before you go blowing anyone's head off, be sure you have good reason." Red was dead serious.

Mitchell nodded, knowing he had probably gone a little too far. But he wasn't going to let anything happen to Beau and Jessica. They had brought the sun back into his life, and he didn't think he could live without their warmth again. "Fine. If we see anything, then we'll call right away. Beau, do you and Jessica want to stay at the house? At least we can be together." There was strength in numbers.

"Yes. Once Jessica wakes from her nap, which should be any time, I'll get her fed and changed and then pack some things so she can spend the night. I'd feel better knowing that you aren't alone either. He might have sent me flowers, but I think this message is really meant for you. He delivered the flowers to me probably because he wants you to know that he's aware of our relationship. He wants you to know that he knows."

"But why?" Mitchell asked, confused. None of this made sense. Why didn't Luke just go on with his life rather than come after him after all this time? It made no sense. Mitchell was trying to move on. Why didn't Luke do the same?

"We can speculate all night," Red said as he stood. "Let me look into things and get back to you. Stay together and keep the dogs around you. They'll warn you if anyone comes snooping around." Red smiled and shook hands with each of them before leaving the house.

"I'm sorry about all this. If I had known, I would have called right away when he delivered them." Beau sighed. "It's just that I was so overwhelmed that you sent me flowers. No one has ever done that before. Gerome didn't believe in things like that. When it came to gifts, he was pretty much a complete dunce. The last Christmas we were together, he got me a welding torch. Gerome had decided that he wanted to try new equipment, so he bought me the welding torch that he wanted for work. I got him a beautiful watch. He loved it and wore it all the time. My welding torch immediately disappeared into his studio." Beau sighed and rolled his eyes. "Needless to say, he never sent me flowers, and when I thought you had…." He let his words trail off.

"I wish it had been from me. Luke was the one to send flowers, and they were always yellow roses. It was sort of his 'I'm sorry' calling card." Mitchell wanted to take the flowers from the table and dump them in the trash, but they were too beautiful just to throw away, so he left them where they were. Still, he hated that Luke had managed to intrude on the happiness he was trying to build—that *they* were trying to build. Mitchell sat down to try to think as Jessica fussed in the other room. Beau went to get her, and Mitchell tried to think about what Luke could be up to. "How is she?"

"A little warm," Beau said, carrying her to the kitchen. She snuffled for a few minutes and then stopped abruptly, probably because of a bottle. "I hope she isn't coming down with something." He felt her forehead and left to get a thermometer to check her temperature, which he reported as normal. She seemed happy enough now that she was being fed. "You said that the roses were always something he sent when he was apologizing. So maybe he's doing that now."

Mitchell thought it over and shrugged. "Except whenever he was apologizing to me, he always brought the flowers himself and gave me his big puppy-dog eyes and promised that he would never do it again, and then he would say he loved me. Luke could be one hell of a conniver when he wanted to be. He would put on music and maybe make a nice meal. He was always sorry and put a lot into his apologies, and then a little while later, all that would be forgotten and I was back on the emotional roller coaster. At first I thought it was me and that I was just not good enough for him. So I tried harder to be the best I could, to do what he wanted and not make him mad. That never worked. It took a long time before I came to realize that it was him. He was the one with the problem, and the only way I was going to be happy was to go. He was angry and got fisty, and I left as soon as I could get away."

"So no flowers after that last time."

"Nope. Like I said, the next time I saw him was at the bookstore. I stayed away from him as best I could, and after that, I never saw him again. I haven't in all these years actually seen him. He sent me cards and letters, but I ripped them to shreds. I didn't want anything from him, and I still don't, other than for him to leave me alone." Mitchell was so over this guy.

"Okay. So maybe he's sending the flowers after all this time. Maybe it took him this long to find you," Beau offered.

Mitchell didn't think that was the case. He hadn't been that hard to find over the past few years.

Jessica watched him, and he placed his finger in her hand. She gripped it tightly while the two dogs settled on the sofa, with Randi right near Jessica, on guard the way she always seemed to be.

"And maybe he's just trying to send a message that he can get to the people in my life. Luke was always at his best when he was in control. It was the times when things got away from him that he got short and upset." Mitchell just wished he could understand what was behind all this so he could make sense on it. "Still, I meant what I said. I'll stand between him and the two of you no matter what."

Beau clicked his tongue. "You don't need to throw yourself on any swords for us, and I certainly don't want you shooting anyone. The thought of having a gun in the house scares the hell out of me." Beau was being honest, and Mitchell understood that.

"I need to keep us all safe. The gun is out of sight and yet in a place I can easily get it if we need it. I can show you where it is if you want."

Beau shook his head. "I don't think I want to know, and yet I probably should. I think happening upon it would scare me more than knowing." He seemed to think a minute. "Yes, you should show me where it is." He seemed to sit a little straighter.

"Have you ever shot a gun?" Mitchell asked.

Beau nodded. "I did when I was a teenager. My dad loved to hunt and things like that. I wasn't really interested in that sort of thing. But he used to take me, and I went because it made him happy. Eventually he figured it out and he went hunting with his buddies and didn't ask me to go anymore. I've shot rifles and handguns because Dad insisted I learn." Beau leaned forward. "I remember going hunting with Dad. We were supposed to bag a deer. I had one in my sights, a prize buck, and Dad was right there with me. The buck was stunning, with eight or ten points, as stately and tall as any I had ever seen." Beau swallowed, and Mitchell couldn't look away from him. "My dad would have been so proud, and all I had to do was take the shot. Instead, I couldn't. He looked so perfect, and the idea of killing him so Dad could mount his head on our wall, and eating him when we had plenty of other food.... I just couldn't pull the trigger. My finger was right there, but it wouldn't happen. Instead, I coughed and made like I couldn't breathe for a second. The deer took off. I lowered the gun, and to my surprise, my dad didn't say anything. Not a single word." Beau looked down at Jessica. "I expected to get yelled at, but he never said anything. He just didn't offer to take me hunting again. I think he knew I could never have pulled the trigger. A target was no problem, but actually shooting something alive… I couldn't do it." Beau didn't lift his gaze away from his daughter. "I haven't touched or fired a gun since."

"I'll show you where it is and how to operate the safety. I keep it on at all times." Mitchell's mind wouldn't stop reeling. He could hardly believe that Luke had returned to his life, and yet he probably should have expected it at some point. Though why now was what puzzled him. There had to have been some change that precipitated it.

His phone vibrated in his pocket, and Mitchell pulled it out, thankful it was Red. "Anything?"

"Something interesting. It seems your friend Luke got himself involved with a man in Delaware, and he wound up in prison for multiple assaults. He got paroled a few months ago."

Mitchell could barely believe it. "You mean he was in prison? For how long?"

"Three years," Red answered. "Which would explain why he was out of the picture for so long. And there's the possibility that he had some time to stew over everyone he might perceive himself as having a grudge with."

"But if he was away for three years and just got out, why would he be coming after me and not the guy who sent him to prison?" Mitchell didn't understand it.

Red cleared his throat. "This is only a theory, but I suspect that person is being protected. He would have testified. If I were a betting man, I'd say that Luke transferred all his anger and bile onto you. You were the one who got away. The one he couldn't reach for a long time."

Maybe that was grasping at straws, but it was as good an explanation as any. Luke wasn't the most emotionally stable person in the world, and if he had spent years ruminating over Mitchell and blaming him for everything that happened to him, regardless of whether it was true, he would likely come to believe it. "It's a possibility."

"Guys in prison get their heads all messed up all the time. It isn't a party, that's for sure. Luke wasn't in one of the worst places, but even medium security can be really rough. I contacted the sheriff's department and explained that it's likely that Luke has violated his probation, and I used a couple of his Facebook pictures as part of the bulletin. I also have a message in to his parole officer. He needs to know if Luke is making trips he shouldn't. We'll keep an eye out for him, and so will the sheriff's department. You guys watch carefully and don't wait to call if you see anything."

"We'll phone right away." They ended the call, and Mitchell explained everything to Beau. "Let's get your things together and lock up the house. We'll bring the dogs to my place, and I want to set up some security on the shelter. If Luke got in there once, he may do it again." Mitchell wasn't sure what he was going to do, but he sure as hell was going to keep his heart safe… and that meant protecting Beau and Jessica, no matter what.

Chapter 12

BEAU GOT Jessica settled in her swing near Mitchell's sofa. The two dogs sat nearby watching her bounce and play, their heads bobbing as she bounced up and down. Beau had already set up her portacrib, and Jessica seemed happy. Too bad Beau couldn't get rid of the knot in his stomach.

Mitchell seemed just as jumpy and couldn't sit still. At the moment, he was out at the shelter, putting up something that he hoped would alert them if anyone tried to get inside. Beau wasn't sure about any of this. Oh, he was pretty sure that Luke was behind what had been happening. But if the guy was smart, he also had to know that they knew—and that he should just get out of town. God, that circle of thought made Beau's head ache.

Mitchell had shown him where he kept the gun, in the top drawer of his desk under a file folder full of papers. Beau hated that it was there, but this was Mitchell's house, and he understood that it was for their protection. Beau only hoped that Luke didn't know where it was too.

"You happy, sweetheart?" he asked, talking to Jessica because he needed something to do to keep his nerves from getting the better of him. Beau didn't think he would be able to sleep much until Luke was out of commission and they were all safe and could go back to their normal lives.

Normal. Beau let the word roll in his head. Nothing had been normal in weeks, and for the most part, he was grateful for that. Before Mitchell came into his life, it was dull and he was alone with Jessica all the time, worrying about Gerome and what he would do next.

Mitchell came inside, locked the door behind him, and sat down on the sofa. "I don't know how much good it will do, but I was able to replace the light outside with a motion-activated one, so if anyone comes through the yard, all the lights should go on." Ruffy bounded over, and Mitchell lifted him onto his lap. "I just want to know what it is he thinks he's going to accomplish. Why couldn't Luke just get on with his life?"

Beau shrugged. "What life? Whatever he had before he went to prison is over. The opportunities for someone like him are very limited, and no matter what happens, he's going to find it hard to get a job or hold one for very long. All his old friends are going to distance themselves, and even his family is going to treat him with suspicion."

"Yeah, maybe. But this isn't going to help with any of that. And if Red is right and he violated his parole, then when they find him, it's right back to prison." Mitchell didn't sound excited. "But that's only after they catch him."

"Then what do we do otherwise?"

Mitchell shrugged. "I'm just a vet, not a security guard or a cop. Red knows what's going on and he's trying to help. But the best thing we can do is try to protect ourselves."

"Not more guns." Beau hated that idea. "I can't stand any more of those things. What if Luke finds it and uses it against us?" He swallowed hard.

"I only have the one gun, and you know where it is," Mitchell said firmly. "I'm not turning my house into an armed fortress, but I don't want you or Jessica to get hurt. Luke has been playing with us up until now. He tried to hurt Randi and opened the dogs' enclosures. By sending the flowers, he might as well have signed the card with his own name."

"Maybe Luke is just trying to watch us squirm," Beau offered. He had been thinking about it. "He's obviously been watching us. You found evidence of him in my shed, but nothing here."

Mitchell paused. "Maybe I should check again." He didn't really seem to like the idea, and Beau certainly didn't.

"You want to wander around the property alone and see if someone might be hiding out there? What will you do if you find him?" He crossed his arms over his chest. "Shoot first and ask questions later?"

"Hey, I wasn't suggesting I get trigger-happy." He shook his head. "I'm sorry if you're a little uncomfortable, but I feel better knowing I have the means to defend us if it's needed. I certainly hope it isn't." Mitchell stilled and then went to the window. The dogs in the shelter were raising quite a ruckus. Mitchell listened and then hurried to the door.

"Be careful."

"I will. Call the police if I'm not back in ten minutes." Mitchell checked his watch and hurried out of the house.

Beau hated this—these times when he sat back inside while Mitchell was out looking into whatever was happening. This was becoming a regular occurrence. Still, he couldn't leave Jessica alone. It made logical sense, but he would have felt better if he could be there to watch Mitchell's back.

Beau wandered to the window overlooking the yard. Mitchell emerged from the shelter and headed across the yard. He suddenly fell to the ground and lay still. Beau wondered what happened and was about to hurry out to check when Mitchell crouched down and raced toward the house. He came inside, slammed the door, and leaned against it, breathless.

"What happened? Are you okay? Did you fall?"

"No. I thought there was a gunshot. I feel like a complete idiot." Mitchell took a deep breath and released it.

"I didn't hear anything," Beau said.

"It wasn't. Just an old truck backfiring on the road. I think it was John Harper's. That thing burns more oil than gas and makes more noise than a popcorn popper. I guess I was a little jumpy. It sounded like a shot and scared me half to death." Mitchell closed his eyes, and Beau moved closer, hugging him tightly. This entire situation had them both on edge. Hopefully it would be over soon. But he knew this wasn't going to resolve on its own.

"We have to bring this to an end. We're both running scared and are as jumpy as cats." He continued holding Mitchell, wishing he had some grand idea that would flush Luke out so he could be turned over to the police. Beau hoped that then maybe he and Mitchell could figure things out between them.

"I know. But this isn't my thing. I keep dogs and cats healthy. I'm not an investigator." He swore. "Maybe if I hadn't messed things up earlier with the poison and in the shelter, we might have had a chance."

"All that might have done was tell us it was Luke before. Now we know." Beau held Mitchell's hand and guided him back toward the sofa. "You dated him for quite a while. What was he like, other than the hot and cold? What kinds of things did he hate? What did he like? Was he a drinker?"

Mitchell nodded. "I don't know what good it could be to anyone. Luke loved good food. He was a terrible cook, but he liked that I could cook and when I made meals for him. Though his favorite times were when we went out, especially…." Mitchell paused. "Especially if someone else was paying."

"Okay. That really doesn't help."

"No…." Mitchell paused again. "But this might. Luke isn't a very patient person. He doesn't sit around and draw things out. At least not the person I knew."

"Which means he's either changed… or something is going to happen soon." That wasn't a good thing at all.

"That seems about right to me. Which is part of what has me bothered. This has been going on for a while, and the only indication that it's him was the flowers. I think he was playing his little game, but we weren't going along. So he had to let me know in his own way that he was behind it." Mitchell leaned against him. "I only wish I knew what his game was. What the hell does he want? It isn't like I'm going to go back to him or let him push me around. I'm not a kid any longer."

Beau paused. "But he doesn't know that. If Luke has been in prison, then the image that he has of you hasn't changed. He still sees you as the same guy he used to hit and push around. Maybe that's the problem. I know this is going to be hard, but somehow you have to face him and let him see the man you are now. The one who stood in front of a police officer and told him that you'd kill an attacker before letting anything happen to me." Beau had been really impressed, and he turned to Mitchell. He knew this wasn't the best time, but….

"What is it?" Mitchell asked quietly, and Beau tugged him into a kiss. He wasn't soft or tentative but demanding and strong. Maybe the intrigue got to him a little, but he leaned forward and pressed

Mitchell down onto the cushions. "Where did this come from?"

"Does it matter?" Beau asked, and Mitchell hummed. Then Beau cupped Mitchell's cheeks, stared into his huge eyes for just a second, and slotted his mouth over Mitchell's, taking his lips with everything he had.

"Not that I'm complaining, but…." Mitchell breathed deeply.

Beau wound his arms around Mitchell's neck. "Then quit talking," he chastised. "We have so many things we could be doing other than that." He climbed on top of Mitchell, straddling him, rocking his hips as he kissed Mitchell harder and harder. Something inside him must have snapped, because he was suddenly ravenous and he couldn't get enough. Mitchell wrapped his arms around him, holding on tightly as Beau vibrated with energy.

Jessica cried from the corner, and Beau groaned as he backed away. His daughter had impeccable timing. "Go and get her." Beau nodded as Mitchell squeezed him. "Once she's in bed and the house is all secured, then you and I will pick up where we left off, I promise."

Beau nodded, unable to trust that his voice wasn't going to break or that he wasn't going to let loose a torrent of frustrated curses. He climbed off the sofa and went to get Jessica, who stopped crying as soon as she saw him. "Hey, sweetheart." He lifted her out of the portacrib and changed her diaper, then carried her to the living room, where he passed her to Mitchell for a cuddle while he went to make up a bottle.

When he returned, Jessica was staring at Mitchell as he sang to her. It was so beautiful and touched his heart in a way nothing else had.

"Do you know what Gerome first told me when he found out I was going to keep Jessica? He said that I would never find a guy who would want someone with a child. That I was dooming myself to a life with just her for company."

Mitchell shook his head and sighed. "What did you tell him?"

Beau smiled. "That I would rather just have Jessica for company than him, and that I thought he was full of crap." He sat down next to Mitchell, who leaned against him. "I would have spent the rest of my life with Jessica as my family."

Mitchell smiled. "You won't have to." He scooted closer, and Beau handed him the bottle. Mitchell fed her, and Jessica held his hand as Mitchell held the bottle. "You know you already have me wrapped around your little finger, don't you?" Mitchell whispered, and Beau rested his head on Mitchell's shoulder. This was always how he had seen himself… his family. But Beau didn't dare let his hopes get too high. Not that Mitchell wasn't a wonderful man—he was. "Yes, you do, sweetie," Mitchell said, continuing to talk to Jessica as Beau ruminated on his own worries. He needed desperately to let go of what Gerome had done.

"Huh?" Beau asked when he realized Mitchell was talking to him. "I'm sorry."

"I was asking what you're thinking about. You were suddenly a long way away." Mitchell took the bottle from Jessica and put her on his shoulder, patting her back to burp her.

"I keep wondering if I'm making the right decision. If I'm capable of making a good decision when it comes to relationships, or if I'm always going to make crap ones."

"You too?" Mitchell asked, and Beau instantly felt better. "It's just another thing our exes took from us. I'm always wondering if what I'm feeling is real and if I can trust it. I was wrong about Luke, and you were wrong about Gerome." He chuckled as Jessica made one of her drunken burps, and Mitchell wiped her face and repositioned her for the rest of her bottle. "We have to leave them behind. It's hard, but we have to be able to trust ourselves again, otherwise we'll never be able to have normal lives. The ones we deserve." Mitchell bumped his shoulder lightly. "Look, you and I didn't do anything wrong. We were the victims of abusers. It's that simple. Yet they go on, and we suffer." Mitchell took the empty bottle from Jessica and burped her once again.

"I think we both have to learn to trust ourselves. This little one trusts us, and I think the two of us have to do that too. Babies know who they can trust, just like dogs. They have a sixth sense for that sort of thing." Beau leaned close and kissed Mitchell gently. "I'm going to choose to trust you and stop all this doubting. I'm just so tired of it. Besides, you've been here when I was being threatened, and you came to little Randi's rescue."

"Of course I did, and I need to do the same. I trust you. That isn't the issue. It's trusting myself." Mitchell turned toward him. "I thought I was doing really well and had worked through my issues with Luke. Then I met you, and they all came back."

"I see."

Mitchell shook his head. "No, I don't think you do. I want things to work out between us. It's important to me, so I keep second-guessing myself. And I hate it, because you're so much better than Luke ever was." He seemed so earnest. "But sometimes it's like he's looking over my shoulder, and I so want to banish him forever and move ahead with my life… with you." Mitchell bit his lower lip. "I know it's pretty soon and I'm taking a chance here, but…."

"I know how you feel." Things with Gerome had happened pretty quickly too, but this felt right and very different. His belly had those excited flutters, but there was none of the trepidation and the worry over whether he was good enough. "I think I get it now."

"Get what?" Mitchell asked as he held Jessica, rocking gently.

"The thing I've been missing." He shifted slightly. "When I started with Gerome, it was all hot and heavy, and everything was so important, and there was this rush of emotion that burned so quick. And this is different."

"O-kay," Mitchell said warily.

Beau realized what he'd said and wanted to sink in the sofa. "I didn't mean that you aren't all those things. With Gerome that was *all* we had. Everything was this heat and passion, with nothing underneath. I can see that now." He took a second to try to collect his thoughts. "Gerome was hot; he still is. That's not to say that you aren't, because later, I intend to burn up the sheets showing you how hot you can be. But that was all there was. I liked that he was a struggling artist. It was cool, and he would sometimes work in nothing but a pair of shorts when it was hot in the summer. It was fun—*he* was fun—until it wasn't, and by then there was nothing left between us except his mood swings, selfishness, and me being scared of him all the damned time." He leaned closer, watching Jessica play and smile. "I think…." He was trying to put how he felt into words and failing. Beau was starting to think that maybe he had made a fool of himself. "I'm not scared with you. I've seen how you are with the dogs and with Jessica. You smile at her the way I always thought that her papa might smile." Okay, maybe he was getting a little sappy and he needed to back off.

Mitchell settled Jessica back into the crook of his arm, and she held his finger as her blue eyes shone brightly. "I know how you feel. Things feel right between us. I've been worrying about the same stuff. And I still am, but for different reasons. It seems my past is still out there, and I have no idea where it's going to strike or what the hell it wants."

He swallowed and rested his head on Beau's shoulder once again. "This is going to sound weird, but when we first met, I thought that maybe you were the one who needed my help. Gerome was hanging around, and…." He chuckled nervously. "I thought I was going to be the white knight and be the one to ride in and protect you and Jessica. But I think I'm the one who needs rescuing. You've moved on from Gerome and largely put him behind you. I thought after five years that I had it together."

Beau nodded. "So you still worry about your ex after all this time. The guy is hanging around trying to hurt our dogs and damage the shelter. He's been watching us and even sending flowers like some demented stalker. Of course you're going to be worried about him. So what? Do you want to get back with him?"

Mitchell shivered. "God, no. Not in a million years."

"And do you miss him or wish the two of you were still friends?" Beau cocked his eyebrows, already knowing the answer.

"You have to be kidding."

"So what it sounds like to me is that you need some closure. I got my chance to tell Gerome goodbye and that I didn't want him back, and that he should go on with his life because I'm going to move ahead with mine. You never got that. And maybe you will and maybe you won't. The thing is to give yourself closure," Beau explained. "In the movies, there's always this grand moment where the hero gets to stand up to their tormentor and overcomes their fear. Sometimes it's just to tell the other guy no… but sometimes—and these are the best—they get to knee the jerk in the privates, and he falls to the ground writhing in pain and agony."

Mitchell put his hand up. "I'll take one of those with a side of discernable limp."

Beau chuckled lightly. "But this isn't one of those movies. And we all don't get to stand up to our tormentors. Sometimes they go away and we have to find our own way and make our own closure."

Mitchell rolled his eyes and looked cute doing it. "What am I supposed to do, write him a letter and then burn it?"

"Yeah, right. Just let yourself be happy. Don't carry Luke around with you in your pocket. He can do what he likes and be as creepy and weird as he wants, but it doesn't change the person you are. He doesn't get to have an effect on you. Whatever he wants or however he acts, it's not a reflection on you, just him."

"But he's still out there," Mitchell protested.

"And one way or another, with Red's help, he'll be found and go back where he belongs. It will be that simple. The guy violated his probation, and no judge is going to look favorably on that, especially once they learn that he did it to stalk someone he'd hurt in the past." Beau hoped Mitchell understood what he was saying.

"I'll try," Mitchell agreed.

"Give yourself a little time to come to terms with what's going on and process it. If Gerome were behind all this, I probably would feel the same way you do. But he's moving on with his life, I'm doing the same, and you can too. Because I want to move on with my life… with you."

Mitchell hummed softly and put his arm around Beau's shoulder. It was nice, and the house was quiet. Jessica was asleep, and they all sat quietly. Beau had no idea how long this moment would last, and he intended to make the very most of it.

"Well, isn't this just an adorable picture?"

Mitchell jumped at the voice behind them. Beau turned as the man who had delivered the flowers stepped into the living room from the kitchen. "I knew if I just waited here long enough you two would scamper over here to be close to the dogs and shit." Randi growled, and Ruffy barked sharply, both of them scampering to get down.

"Shut up your dust mops, or I'll lock them in the basement."

"You must be Luke," Beau said as he took Jessica and held her close. She had started to cry, and Beau did his best not to shiver at the piece of cold steel that Luke pointed at Mitchell.

"And you must be the daddy," Luke sneered. "Just stay where you are. Both of you."

"Just stop it," Mitchell demanded. "What the hell are you doing here, anyway? Why didn't you just stay away? What is it that you want? I haven't seen you in five years, and suddenly you're back, watching us, trying to hurt the dogs. What's gotten into you?" he asked as he stood. "Oh for God's sake, put the gun away." He put his hands on his hips. "I'm the one who should be angry with you for how you treated me."

"How I treated you?" Luke asked. "You got what you deserved, what you wanted. I know you only egged me on because you loved it."

Beau went cold and held Jessica tighter, trying to soothe her into being quiet while he figured out a way to get to the phone in his pocket.

"No, I didn't. And I left you because of it. You've had years to go on with your own life, and that's what you need to do. You and I haven't been together in a long time. Why do you want me now?" Mitchell asked.

Luke stalked closer to him and pushed Mitchell back hard enough that he practically fell onto the sofa. "I don't want you. I want your little life here with your boyfriend and the baby. I want your family, the one I can't have." He was more than a little off his nut. His eyes were huge, and the hand that held the gun shook slightly. This was terrible and…. Beau wrinkled his nose at the smell that rose from Jessica's diaper. Oh God, she had to pick right now to….

"Take care of the little squawker, but don't you dare try anything, or the part of little Mitchell's family that I take first is her," he growled.

Beau nodded and slowly got up.

"I have to get the diapers out of the bag." He pointed to the side of the sofa and slowly moved in that direction. Using the movement as cover, he got his phone out of his pocket and slipped it into the diaper bag as he reached for a clean diaper. Then he held it up and set it on the cushions. "I just need the wipes." He reached again for the bag, pressed 911 on the phone, grabbed the wipes, and hoped to all hell that would be enough to get them some help.

He showed Luke the wipes and spread a pad on the sofa cushions, then changed and cleaned Jessica as quickly as he could. Beau hated the thought of Luke seeing his daughter while he was changing her, and Mitchell slid over to stand in front of him.

"What are you doing?" Luke snapped.

"Letting Beau change her. What, do you get your jollies out of naked babies?" Mitchell challenged.

Beau jumped at the loud slap, but he finished changing Jessica and got her dressed.

"You think you can get me to do what you want by hitting? That isn't going to work anymore. I don't love you and am not interested in you in any way. I carried you around with me for a long time." Mitchell brushed at each shoulder. "But you're gone now, so take the hint and get out of here. Leave us alone and go on with your life."

"I can't," Luke growled. "My life is gone, and it's because of lying guys like you. I never did anything to anyone that they didn't want or deserve. You little shits lie about everything afterwards, and I spent three years in prison because of it." He stalked nearer, and Beau held Jessica as closely as he could, turning away to try to protect her from Luke, even as Mitchell stood in front of them.

Damn, he was like a knight in armor, standing between them and danger. "I had nothing at all to do with what happened to you. I finished my work and set myself up in a practice here. I never came to see you, and I wasn't contacted by anyone about you. I didn't even know what had happened to you. I thought you had moved on, and I was doing the same." Mitchell's voice was calm, even though Beau could see the tension in his ramrod-straight back. "Why are you here? What did I ever do to you?"

Luke growled. "You know what the fuck you did. You left and turned all the other guys I dated against me. I know it was you. Then you got that little shit to lie about me in court and to the police, and they put me in prison. Do you know what happens to guys in prison?" he practically shouted, and the dogs raced from the room. Not that Beau could blame them. Beau could practically smell the scent of fear and loathing that filled the room, like the musty scent of old fire that lingered in the air.

"No. I've never been there," Mitchell said gently. "And I'm sorry if bad things happened to you, but I had nothing to do with them, and neither did Beau or the baby." He looked at Luke, his eyes burning, lips a straight line. Beau saw the same helplessness that filled him—Mitchell was seeking an answer the same as Beau was.

"Being used like that for months hurt, and there was nothing I could do about it. Not a thing. No one gave a damn, not you, not any of the people I thought loved me. No one. My only visitor in three years was my mother, and she came exactly twice." Luke's hand shook even more, and rage filled his eyes. This was going to end badly, Beau knew it.

"But that wasn't us. We didn't hurt you. I never hurt anyone; you know that. Remember when we were dating and I found that squirrel in the woods and tried to help it? I couldn't let a squirrel suffer. I certainly wouldn't hurt another person." Damn, that was brilliant. Mitchell was getting Luke back to a happier time, one that was less stressful, and getting him to remember how kind Mitchell was at the same time.

Luke still held his gun on Mitchell. "Don't try that shit. I…."

"What, Luke? What are you going to do? Shoot me? Shoot Beau and a baby? Really? I know you better than that. You aren't a killer." He continued talking softly. "You need to think about what you're going to do. What is it you're hoping to get out of all this? I'm not coming back to you, and nothing is going to be like it was. No matter what." He didn't look away, and Beau could see Luke faltering. Whatever he was thinking, Mitchell had been able to instill doubt and worry. "Luke, just turn around and go home. This isn't going to turn out well. You have to be able to see that." Mitchell moved away, and Beau turned his head to the side, listening intently.

Sirens sounded just on the edge of his hearing and grew louder and more urgent. "You called the fucking police!" Luke shouted. "Why the fuck did you do that?" The sirens grew louder as the cars pulled into the drive, their lights shining through the windows.

"Just relax. They're here now, and all you need to do is put the gun down." Mitchell's voice was strained.

"They won't do anything as long as I have the three of you," Luke said.

"Please. How many television shows have you watched?" Beau pointed out.

"Mitchell, Beau, are you all right?" Red's voice came through a loudspeaker.

"No!" Beau shouted. "We need help." Luke raced forward, and Mitchell slammed into him, pushing Luke off balance. He fell to the floor, still holding the gun. Mitchell raced to where he had his gun, grabbed it from the desk drawer, and pointed it at Luke.

"It's over. Don't you dare move or so help me, I'll blow your head off," Mitchell yelled, but Beau could see the way his hands shook, and he knew that Mitchell was contemplating the possibility that he might have to shoot someone. Luke saw it too—he must have, because he sneered, and Beau knew, seconds before either of them moved, that something was about to happen and that Luke was just crazy enough to test Mitchell's resolve. He braced for what was to come next and did his best to protect Jessica.

Luke put both hands together and swung, knocking Mitchell's hand away. Then he pushed into Mitchell, the two of them fighting for Luke's gun. A shot rang out in the room, and Jessica began wailing as the dogs yowled and barked. Beau held his breath as he wondered if Mitchell had been shot. Blood bloomed between the two men, and Beau tried to figure out who had shot whom. Mitchell moved and lifted away from Luke. "Mitchell!"

"I'm okay." He jumped up and ran to the door. "Please get in here. Luke has been shot." He stood out of the way as the police swarmed inside. They secured Mitchell as well as Luke. Beau attempted to clarify to the police who the trespasser was, and they let Mitchell go as ambulance personnel came inside.

"How bad is it?" Mitchell asked as the EMTs worked.

"He was shot in the shoulder, so he's really lucky," one of the EMTs said as they continued working. They eventually took Luke out of the house.

It was then that the questions began in earnest. Beau explained what happened as best he could. Mitchell did the same.

"You're very lucky you weren't shot," the deputy told Mitchell. Beau didn't meet Mitchell's gaze because he didn't want an "I told you so" moment, but he couldn't help thinking it. "People think having a gun in their house will save them."

"There was already a gun in the house. Luke had one of his own." Beau pointed to where it had slid under the sofa. "We were all lucky. I managed to call 911 when he thought I was getting diapers out of the bag." Beau grabbed his phone and closed the app.

"That was you? We weren't sure what was going on until Mitchell got him to talk. The operator heard everything, and she got in touch with us."

Beau soothed Jessica, who was very fussy and crying out of fear. Randi and Ruffy both jumped up onto the sofa, with Randi taking up a guard position for her baby.

Mitchell left the room and returned with a clean shirt, handing the one he'd worn to the deputy in case it was needed. Then he sat next to Beau, doing his best to soothe Jessica. It wasn't until Mitchell began to sing softly that the little one quieted. "You're developing the magic voice."

Mitchell nodded and closed his eyes. "As long as we're all safe. That's what counts." He scooted closer. "I can't believe I did that."

"What? Work to piss Luke off… then nearly talk him down… or maybe wrestle him for the gun and nearly give me a complete heart attack? Take your pick, they're all equally frightening." Beau's heart finally stopped pounding so hard that his chest felt like it was going to explode.

"I'm sorry. I guess I had some issues I needed to work through, and I couldn't let anything happen to you and Jessica." Mitchell smoothed his hand over her head. "That was real smart, the way you called for help."

"I didn't know what else to do. All I could do was dial and hope they understood that we needed assistance." He leaned against Mitchell, breathing as regularly as he could. "We'll all be okay," he repeated a few times.

Now that it was over, all the tension and worry that had built up over the past week or so came to the surface, and Beau wiped his eyes before burying his face against Mitchell. There were still police officers in the house, and he didn't want them to see him go to pieces, but that was what was happening and he couldn't help it. The thought of anyone hurting his daughter was too much for him, and he shook almost uncontrollably.

"It's okay," Mitchell whispered. "Just let it out."

"Are you okay?" Red asked as he sat across from them.

"We will be," Mitchell answered for both of them. "He came in through the back door and just walked in the house as bold as anything."

"Did he say why he was so obsessed with you?" Red asked gently.

Beau lifted his face and wiped his eyes. "He wasn't completely coherent, but he blamed Mitchell for what had happened to him. He said that it was guys like Mitchell who were responsible for his getting into trouble and going to prison." He shook his head and sniffed. "It was like everything was someone else's fault. I don't think he could get at the guy who testified against him, so he came after Mitchell. I guess he lumped all his victims together in his mind."

"That makes sense," Red said, and both Beau and Mitchell stiffened. "His parole officer said that he was concerned about Luke and had required that he go to counseling. But it looks like that never happened. It seems that everyone was worried about his mental health, and there's speculation about whether his parole should ever have been granted at all." He rubbed the back of his neck. "His officer said that Luke's parents were putting on a lot of pressure, and I think that may have had some influence on what happened." He shook his head. "His parole officer has asked for a copy of the report. I think he means to stick it to some of the decision-makers."

"Will he go back to prison?" Beau asked.

"I'm not sure."

Mitchell sighed. "He needs help, so a prison hospital is probably a better choice, but I know we don't get any say. But he needs to be kept away for everyone's safety. The guy needs a lot of help." He seemed like the wind had gone out of his sails.

"I hope that happens. But it's out of our hands now. Charges will be filed here. Delaware is going to want him returned. The prosecutors will need to work things out. Either way, he isn't going to be around to bother you, or anyone else, for quite some time." Red turned as a deputy joined them. "This is Pierre. He's a deputy with the sheriff's department, and he'll take your statements. Once that's done, we should be finished here."

Mitchell nodded and remained quiet. The police finished their work, and Beau managed to soothe Jessica to sleep. "I need to check on a few things," he said quietly and handed Jessica to Mitchell. Not that Beau really had anything to do, but he thought Mitchell might need a little of Jessica's sweetness right at that moment. He left the house and walked past the police officers and the car where Luke sat on the ground waiting for the ambulance and headed toward the barn.

He pushed the door open and was greeted by a bevy of dogs, most wagging their tails and barking excitedly from their enclosures. "Your daddy is okay." He walked around to each one and bent down to greet them and receive licks. Beau took a deep breath and put his hands over his face, the tears coming in waves that he couldn't seem to stop.

"What are you doing here?" Mitchell asked, Jessica asleep in his arms.

"I guess I needed a few minutes," Beau whispered. "And I knew these guys wouldn't judge me if I cried like a baby." He leaned against one of the wooden supports, using it to keep him on his feet. "We were held at gunpoint by a crazy man. How can you be so damned composed about it?"

"I guess because I have you," Mitchell said. "And maybe I finally got what I want. Luke is out of my life, and I got to tell him that I was done." He almost smiled. "I know it sucks how it happened, but I got closure. Luke is gone, and no matter what I might remember from before, it's over with now. And whatever we may have been or however he may have treated me, I got the better of him in the end." He sighed. "Come here and hold your daughter."

It seemed they were passing her back and forth. Beau took her, and almost instantly the ground under his feet seemed to firm.

"She's okay, so are you and I, and all the dogs are fine. The world is back on its axis and is still turning the way it should."

Beau snorted. "Sometimes you say the strangest things."

"Yeah, I know. But I have what's most important." Mitchell held Beau's gaze. "I have you two. That's all that matters. That is, if you want me." He shifted his weight from foot to foot. "I know we just met a few weeks ago and things have started off with a trial by fire… but I was hoping that now that things can be quieter, maybe you and I can go on a few dates and in a few months show Jessica her first snow." Mitchell faltered and turned away. "And maybe I just want too much." He fiddled with the latch on the door of one of the dog enclosures. "I'm doing it again, aren't I? Jumping in with both feet too soon."

Beau put his hand on Mitchell's shoulder. "I want that too. I want to see where this goes. You and I have been through a lot in the past few weeks, and maybe we can sort of work through our issues together." He steadied his voice. "I guess I've come to accept that I don't have things as together as I thought I did."

Jessica cooed softly, and Mitchell turned toward her. He grinned, and Jessica smiled right back at him before putting her hand in her mouth. "Look at you… all smiley."

"Yeah," Mitchell agreed. "I always wanted someone to smile at me like that." Beau knew exactly how he felt and leaned closer. Jessica seemed to giggle as Mitchell kissed Beau. It was too soon for anything else, but for right now Beau would take the quiet of just the two of them… and a shelter full of dogs. Okay, maybe not so quiet. Beau knew darned well that from now on his life was going to be full of family, both Jessica and the four-legged kind, and it sounded absolutely perfect to him.

Epilogue

THE HARVEST Festival of the Arts was going great guns, with people packing the main street of Carlisle to sample the wares of a hundred artists, scarf down amazing junk food, and just be seen. Mitchell stood in the middle of his double booth with the dogs on leashes or in pens, happy as anything.

The last few months had gone very well. Their lives had quieted and Beau had sold the house and studio in Philadelphia for more than he expected. Sometimes Mitchell wondered if things were going too well, but he wasn't going to question being happy. He didn't have time for daydreaming and pulled his attention back where it belonged.

"She's so cute, Daddy," a little girl said as she cradled Chester, a terrier mix, who snuggled right in like he was made for her. "Can we get him, please?"

Mitchell had seen those eyes so many times today. Every kid wanted a dog, and so many of them had stopped by to hold or pet one of his.

"He's really good with kids," Beau said from the corner of the booth where he held Jessica. She was right at the point where she was starting to pull herself up.

The father looked indecisive as the little girl petted Chester and started talking to him. "Okay, Pumpkin. I promised you a puppy for your birthday." He smiled and turned to Mitchell. "At least I won't have to go through the puppy phase."

"Chester is about two, and he's all up to date on his shots. All the dogs are." Mitchell handed the father a sheet to fill out.

"Is there a cost for the dog?" He took the form and started completing it.

"We only charge what it cost for housing, medical care, and feeding the dogs. I have a veterinary practice west of town, and the shelter is an offshoot of that. A lot of our dogs are rescued from bad situations or were injured and their owners didn't want them any longer. We care for the dogs, nurse them back to health, and then find them good homes." Mitchell smiled as the little girl held Chester, grinning from ear to ear. "We found Chester three months ago in the woods. He had been running wild for some time. Fortunately he's just as loveable and gentle as they come." The poor thing had been miserable when Mitchell had found him. Mitchell didn't need to go into that much detail.

"Thank you, Daddy," the little girl said, and Mitchell took a few minutes to go over how to care for Chester with both of his new owners. He got them a new-dog packet, and the father bought Chester food and supplies from the display that Beau had insisted

Mitchell set up and have ready for the new owners. On his leash, Chester was led away, prancing next to the little girl like he was king of the world.

Mitchell turned away and tried not to make a big deal of wiping his eyes.

"I know those are happy tears," Beau said gently. Finding them homes was wonderful, but saying goodbye was hard for Mitchell. "And you're a great big softie."

"That hasn't changed." Another group of people came into the booth, and Mitchell went to help them. They were older and looking for a companion that would fit into their lives. After five minutes, they settled on Daisy, a middle-aged boxer mix who was perfect for them. They took her away after completing the forms, paying the adoption fee, and nearly buying out the stock of supplies he had left.

"What are we going to do with this sweet girl?" Beau asked, referring to the last dog left, a miniature beagle who was just full of energy. Rosie only had one eye and was partially deaf, but beautiful and loving. Mitchell had been trying to find her a home for months now with no luck.

"Pierre," Beau said as the sheriff's deputy stepped into the booth.

"Hi, Beau. This is my husband, Jordan." They all shook hands. "I've been telling him about your shelter."

"Who's this little one?" Jordan asked as he leaned down.

"Rosie."

He put his fingers near the wire, and she licked them. Mitchell got her out, and Rosie went right into Jordan's arms. He knew instantly that his last rescue of the day had likely found a home. Sure enough, Pierre filled out the forms and left a donation in addition to the adoption fee, and the two of them carried their little girl away.

"That's it, then," Beau said as Jessica squirmed to get down. He put her on her feet, and held her hands to get her used to being upright. The day had been a success in every way Mitchell could have expected. He lifted Jessica into his arms, and she lay against his shoulder. "Should we start to tear down?"

"No. I have brochures, and I'm hoping people will come see our other dogs." The pups they had brought to the booth had all been adopted. Mitchell sat in one of the chairs, with Beau next to him. "We can sit and relax for a little while." He took Beau's hand, and they sat quietly. "Then we can pack up and go home. I have something I want to talk about."

Mitchell smiled as he thought about the small box on top of the dresser that held something he'd gotten for Beau, along with the question he wanted to ask, but that was something he wanted to do when they were alone, just the three of them, their happy family.

ANDREW GREY is the author of more than one hundred works of Contemporary Gay Romantic fiction. After twenty-seven years in corporate America, he has now settled down in Central Pennsylvania with his husband, Dominic, and his laptop. An interesting ménage. Andrew grew up in western Michigan with a father who loved to tell stories and a mother who loved to read them. Since then he has lived throughout the country and traveled throughout the world. He is a recipient of the RWA Centennial Award, has a master's degree from the University of Wisconsin–Milwaukee, and now writes full-time. Andrew's hobbies include collecting antiques, gardening, and leaving his dirty dishes anywhere but in the sink (particularly when writing). He considers himself blessed with an accepting family, fantastic friends, and the world's most suppor supportive and loving partner. Andrew currently lives in beautiful, historic Carlisle, Pennsylvania.

Email: andrewgrey@comcast.net
Website: www.andrewgreybooks.com

BAD
TO BE GOOD
ANDREW GREY

Bad to Be Good: Book One

Longboat Key, Florida, is about as far from the streets of Detroit as a group of gay former mobsters can get, but threats from within their own organization forced them into witness protection—and a new life.

Richard Marsden is making the best of his second chance, tending bar and learning who he is outside of organized crime… and flirting with the cute single dad, Daniel, who comes in every Wednesday. But much like Richard, Daniel hides dark secrets that could get him killed. When Daniel's past as a hacker catches up to him, Richard has the skills to help Daniel out, but not without raising some serious questions and risking his own new identity and the friends who went into hiding with him.

Solving problems like Daniel's is what Richard does best—and what he's trying to escape. But finding a way to keep Daniel and his son safe without sacrificing the person he's becoming will take some imagination, and the stakes have never been higher. This time it's not just lives on the line—it's his heart….

Half a
Cowboy
Andrew Grey

Ever since his discharge from the military, injured veteran Ashton Covert has been running his family ranch—and running himself into the ground to prove he still can.

Ben Malton knows about running too. When he takes refuge in Ashton's barn after an accident in a Wyoming blizzard, he's thinking only of survival and escaping his abusive criminal ex, Dallas.

Ashton has never met a responsibility he wouldn't try to shoulder. When he finds Ben half-frozen, he takes it upon himself to help. But deadly trouble follows Ben wherever he goes. He needs to continue on, except it may already be too late.

Working together brings Ben and Ashton close, kindling fires not even the Wyoming winter can douse. Something about Ben makes Ashton feel whole again. But before they can ride into the sunset together, they need to put an end to Dallas's threats. Ben can make a stand, with Ashton's help—only it turns out the real danger could be much closer to home.

www.dreamspinnerpress.com